MW00770465

Tempest in the Tea Room

A Jewish Regency Mystery

LIBI ASTAIRE

ASTER PRESS

First published 2012
Copyright 2012 by Libi Astaire
Cover photo: Copyright iStockphoto.com/Dimitrije
Tanaskovic

ISBN 978-0-9837931-6-8

Published and distributed by:

Aster Press
Kansas-Jerusalem
www.libiastaire.weebly.com

PROLOGUE

Reader, may I presume that you are also a person of taste and sensibility, and will therefore have interest in events that extend beyond your own familiar circle? I refer, of course, to certain events that have thrown London's Jewish community into turmoil. And I do not refer to the unfortunate incident that occurred at my family's Passover Seder, when a certain six-year-old boy who shall remain nameless produced from his coat pocket a hunk of bread while he was reciting The Four Questions.

Since it is well known that it is forbidden for a Jewish family to have even a crumb of leavened bread in their home during the Passover holiday, much less a piece nearly the size of a small loaf, I shall assume there is no need to describe in great detail what followed. Suffice it to say that the matriarch of our family, Mrs Rose Lyon, first screamed and then gasped for air in a most terrifying manner, before falling into a faint and banging her head against the table—a movement that upset a wine goblet and sent the purpley contents spilling all over the new dress of Miss Esther Lyon, who loudly protested the disturbance to not only her costume but also the gown that had been made before the holiday for her favourite doll, Charlotte.

This commotion quite naturally inspired the newest member of our family circle, Master Isaac Goldsmith, infant (I am an Aunt!), to commiserate with his illustrious grandmother. Isaac broke into a wail that could be heard all the way to Bury Street, I should think, and would not be comforted until his mother, Mrs Hannah Goldsmith, nee Lyon, removed him from the scene of the battlefield.

Meanwhile, the crumblysome situation, which was fast descending into a debacle of the most alarming proportions, was saved by the quick thinking of the patriarch of our family, Mr Samuel Lyon, clockmaker to the fashionable world, who deftly imprisoned the offending piece of bread in the folds of a linen napkin. The napkin was transferred downstairs, where it was safely disposed of by that most excellent of servants, Meshullam Mendel, who had been conducting his own Seder with his wife Sorel and daughter Perl before the ruckus upstairs so unexpectedly interrupted him.

Mrs Lyon was returned to life thanks to the expert ministrations of Mr Gabriel Taylor, a physician newly arrived in London and a guest at our family's Seder. And here, at last, I have come to what I meant to tell you from the first. For the storm at our Seder table was but a mild summer rain in comparison to the gale that enveloped Mr Taylor not long after the Passover holiday had concluded—a veritable typhoon that threatened to not only ruin the young man's career but also send him to the gallows!

Fortunately, Mr Ezra Melamed, the distinguished benefactor of London's Jewish community, once again came to the assistance of a fellow Jew and skillfully aided the young doctor during his hour of need. But when the danger had passed, the question again arose as to who should fulfill the important role of chronicler of this interesting story for future generations.

"Since Miss Rebecca Lyon has shown a talent for writing in the past, I see no reason why she should not set down on paper this story, as well," Mr Melamed declared.

Reader, I hope you will sympathize with the natural feelings of confusion and embarrassment that such an unexpected compliment aroused. I would have liked to have run from the drawing room, so overcome was I by this gratifying mention of my youthful authorly efforts—whose success I must firstly attribute to the One Above whom we Jews refer to as Hashem, and secondly to the edifying influence of that well-known female practitioner of the horrid novel, Mrs Anne Radcliffe—if duty had not forced me to stay my ground and protest mightily that a pen more experienced than mine was needed to do justice to this megillah (a megillah being the story of a Jewish person's near brush with disaster and ultimate salvation by the Guardian of Israel and the true Healer of all souls).

However, my attempts at persuasion were, alas, only as successful as the oratorical attempts of one of Mrs Radcliffe's heroines to free herself from imprisonment in some lonesome and loathsome Italian tower, which is to say they were not successful at all.

Mr Melamed protested that his business and communal concerns precluded him from embarking upon a literary project of such magnitude. Mr Taylor insisted that since he was a physician his acquaintance with the author's art was limited to the writing of medicines, while his sister, Miss Elisheva

Taylor, declared with equal force that her talents lay in other, more homey spheres. Therefore, rather than leave the tale to languish in the dusty, forgetful labyrinths of memory and imagination, I open my writing box and, with many blushes and a fresh supply of ink, begin the tale of *Tempest in the Tea Room*.

Devonshire Square, London, England
Erev Shavuos 5571/May 28, 1811

CHAPTER I

"Re…be…cca! Reh…! Beh…! Beh…! "

"Rebecca, why do you vex the child, when Isaac cannot speak? Your time would be more profitably spent in helping us hem these clothes." Mrs Rose Lyon gave her daughter a disapproving glance and then returned her attention to the tiny dress that sat in her lap.

Rebecca stroked the cheek of her nephew, Master Isaac Goldsmith, age four weeks, to reassure the infant that his inability to articulate the name of his eldest (and surely favourite) aunt was no aspersion on either his intelligence or his affectionate nature. "You want to say my name. I know you do," she whispered. When she was greeted by a smile, or something that seemed very like, she, in turn, was reassured that her high estimation of her only nephew had not been misplaced.

"Give me the dress, Mama, and I will hem it," said the infant's mother, Mrs Hannah Goldsmith. "Rebecca is much better employed in amusing Isaac."

Rebecca could feel the tips of her ears turn red. She dearly loved her older sister, considering Hannah to be everything that a Daughter of Israel should be, but wished that Hannah had not brought up the subject, even subtly, of Rebecca's inability to sew her stitches in an even line.

"She must learn to master the needle," Mrs Lyon said with a heartfelt sigh, plying *her* needle with expert motion. "What will people say when her children enter the Great Synagogue with ragged hems and uneven sleeves?"

"That is still several years away. She has ample time to improve her needlework. The main thing is to want to improve, which I am sure is a thing that Rebecca desires as much as you do. Is that not so, Rebecca?"

Rebecca did not answer at once. The truth was that she much preferred to wield a pen or a paintbrush than a needle, which always seemed to play pranks with her fingers and make the most disconcerting movements on the cloth. When she had heard Mr Franks, the father of her good friend Miss Harriet Franks, discuss with her father a machine that could cut cloth, sew seams and hems, and even produce a tolerable buttonhole, she had begged her father to procure the wonder at once.

"Is such a machine in existence today?" Mr Lyon had asked.

"Oh, I do not speak of today," Mr Franks had replied. "I speak of a future time, when the machine will perform many of the mundane tasks that currently occupy our hours."

At the time, Rebecca had been contented with this answer. Now, however, she silently wondered if that future epoch might occur within the next six or seven years, when she could expect to take her place among the married matrons of London's Jewish community. If so, she would be spared much agony. In the meanwhile, though, she was aware that both her sister and her mother were waiting for her reply.

"Yes, Hannah, I should like to improve. And I am sorry you no longer live with us in Devonshire Square, as I am sure that now that I am older I should make a much better pupil."

"Bury Street is not so very far."

"No, but you are so busy, since you have become a mother."

"I have not the time, it is true, but perhaps Miss Taylor could perform the duties of a teacher."

Mrs Lyon, who had been following the conversation with interest, said with astonishment, "Why should a stranger teach Rebecca sewing, when she has a mother to instruct her?"

"I did not mean to offend, Mama, but I think you will like my little scheme when you hear it."

At that moment the patriarch of the family, Mr Samuel Lyon, entered the drawing room. In place of his usually genial manner, a more serious expression was etched upon his face. "What is this, Hannah? Motherhood should elevate a young lady, not turn her into a schemer or gossip."

"Yes, Papa, but before you judge me, please do me the favour of first hearing what scheme I have planned."

Mr Lyon took his accustomed seat by the hearth and motioned for his eldest child to proceed.

"It has come to my attention that the situation of Mr Taylor and his sister is not all that it should be," Hannah began. "Their rooms are above ours, on Bury Street, as you know, Papa."

Mr Lyon, having unintentionally fallen into the role of judge, nodded his head in what he hoped was a suitably judicial manner.

"Knowing that they are but newly arrived in London, and apparently without family or acquaintances," Hannah continued, "I have on more than one occasion invited Miss Taylor to my apartments for tea. But she has refused my overtures."

"This surprises me," said Mr Lyon. "They accepted our invitation to the Seder. Miss Taylor seemed to be a sensible, well-bred young lady."

"She praised my special recipe for gefilte fish exceedingly," added Mrs Lyon, by way of agreement with her husband.

"I believe she is a well-bred person, as well," Hannah replied, "and that it is only the embarrassment of a too limited income that prevents her from accepting my invitations. If she were to have tea with me, she would feel obligated to invite me in return, and it is my belief that she and her brother do not have enough food for themselves, let alone others."

"I do not understand you, Hannah," said Mrs Lyon. "Is not Mr Taylor employed as physician to the Jewish orphanage? And how can he engage rooms on Bury Street, if he does not possess a comfortable income? The building is owned by Mr Melamed, who maintains his own apartments in the house next door. It is fantastic to suggest that Mr Melamed would let his property to paupers."

Mr Lyon cleared his throat loudly and rose from his seat.

"What are you doing, Mr Lyon?" asked his helpmeet, as she watched him search behind the high-backed settle that stood in a corner of the room.

"Passover has finished. There is no longer a need to search for *chometz*."

"It is not unleavened bread that I am searching for," he replied, turning his attention to the long-case clock and looking inside. Satisfied that the case was empty of all but the workings of the stately clock, he next walked over to the door that led to the library, which he quickly opened and just as quickly closed.

"Then what are you looking for?"

"Joshua," he replied, striding down to the far end of the drawing room, where he opened the door that led to the hall.

"Joshua and Esther and Sarah are in the nursery, in bed."

"In theory, but I wish to be certain."

After casting a careful eye behind the curtains, and finally assuring himself that a certain inquisitive six-year-old boy was not hidden in the room, Mr Lyon returned to his place by the mantelpiece.

"What I am about to say must go no further than these four walls," he began, casting a solemn glance upon each of the ladies in turn. "Mr Taylor and his sister are, indeed, without family or friends. Their parents died of the fever in Jamaica, as I understand, and Mr Taylor used the small legacy he received to undergo training as a physician. I believe he studied somewhere on the Continent."

"If I recall correctly, at the Seder he mentioned that he had studied in Gottingen," said Hannah.

"Why did he study medicine in a German city and not in England?" asked Rebecca.

"There is only one medical school in England that will accept young men of our faith, and places are limited," replied Mr Lyon. "Mr Taylor was not

~ 11 ~

accepted, perhaps because he was neither born nor reared in this country."

Rebecca accepted this answer, but as so often happened, no sooner had one question been resolved than another one rushed into her mind. "I wonder that he did not return to Jamaica, to become a physician there. Jamaica must be very beautiful."

"The island might have its charms for an artist," said Mr Lyon, well aware of his daughter's interest in painting and drawing. "But Mr Taylor has an unmarried sister, and the Caribbean is not the place to find her a suitable husband."

"But if she has no fortune, what good will it do her to be in England?" asked Mrs Lyon, who was always very practical when it came to matrimonial matters.

"Once her brother is established as a physician, Miss Taylor's prospects should improve."

Mrs Lyon remained doubtful. "His work at the orphanage cannot bring him much. Has he other patients?"

"I believe that Mr Melamed engaged his services before Passover. And should anyone in our family require a physician, I have assured Mr Melamed that we shall send for Mr Taylor, as well."

"Thank G-d, our children are healthy - pooh, pooh, pooh," said Mrs Lyon, looking nervously about her to make sure that no demon harbingers of disease had crept into the room. "I should not like to have a physician as a regular visitor to our home, unless, of course, it was to invite Mr Taylor and his sister for a Shabbos meal."

"I only say that should one of our children develop a cough or a sore throat, we would be doing

~ 12 ~

Mr Melamed a favour by sending for Mr Taylor. You, Rebecca, for instance, if I am not mistaken, this evening you are looking a little pale. Are you perhaps not feeling well?"

"I am very well, only I am puzzled. Why would we be doing Mr Melamed a favour by engaging the services of …?" Rebecca suddenly blushed. "Oh, I see. Mr Taylor and his sister are Mr Melamed's current charity case, is that it, Papa?"

"Mr Melamed is most likely letting the rooms on Bury Street for a minimal sum, until Mr Taylor's medical practice is established," said Hannah, taking up the conversation's thread.

"Our Sages tell us that the highest form of charity is to help set up a person in business, so that one day he will no longer need public assistance," said Mr Lyon. "Therefore, it is the responsibility of all of us to help newcomers to our community, not just Mr Melamed."

"But we do not have to make ourselves sick to do so," insisted Mrs Lyon.

"That is why I should like to tell you my scheme, Papa. I have also tried to think of a way to help Mr Taylor and his sister."

"If your intention is to help and not harm, Hannah, I should very much like to hear what you have to say."

"You, Papa, would not notice the expert manner in which Miss Taylor has mended and refashioned her walking costume from last year, but such things do attract a lady's eye. I therefore thought that perhaps she could be employed to teach needlework to Rebecca and Esther and Sarah. We could say that she would be doing us a great favour, since Mama and I are so busy with making bed linen for the baby that we do not have the time to instruct the girls ourselves."

"If Miss Taylor would give her assent, it would be a very good scheme, indeed. Do you not agree, Mrs Lyon?"

"With all my heart," said Mrs Lyon. "Invite Miss Taylor to pay us a call the day after tomorrow, Hannah. I shall inform Mrs Baer."

"Mrs Baer?" Mr Lyon protested. "Surely her duties at the coffee house would prevent her from attending a sewing party."

"I do not like to contradict you, my dear, but I assure you that once Mrs Baer hears that there is an orphaned young lady in London who is in search of a husband, there is nothing that will prevent her from making Miss Taylor's acquaintance."

CHAPTER II

To Rebecca's immense relief, the ladies invited to the sewing party were too busy admiring the skilled alterations that Miss Taylor made to one of Hannah's bonnets to pay much attention to her own attempt to embroider a handkerchief. Mrs Baer, in particular, was effusive with her compliments, and at the first occasion when Miss Taylor was out of earshot, she whispered to Mrs Lyon, "I know just the young man."

"Who?" asked Mrs Lyon, dropping a stitch in her excitement to learn which person had been chosen to be Miss Taylor's future husband.

Should the Reader be surprised that the future happiness of a young lady should be decided by someone who has made her acquaintance only an hour before, it can only be because you are not yet acquainted with the formidable powers of Mrs Baer, a woman in our community who is as well known for her matchmaking abilities as for her delicious kugels, which is saying a great deal. Just as some people have a talent for discovering the interlocking mysteries of nature or the navigational secrets of the star-filled sky, Mrs Baer has been blessed with an uncanny ability to dissect the mystery of a young person's soul and—like the knowledgeable surgeon who knits together a fragmented bone with its fellow—join that soul to the mate who will both appreciate their good qualities and help them to smooth those still jagged edges where improvement is needed.

But before Mrs Baer could deposit the young man's name into Mrs Lyon's waiting ear, Miss Taylor had finished her tour of the china cabinet, where a series of china plates painted by Miss Rebecca Lyon was on display, and retaken her seat.

"You must be very proud of your daughter's talents, Mrs Lyon," she said. "I would give much to be able to paint as well."

Mrs Lyon, unaccustomed to hearing her second daughter so highly praised, was momentarily at a loss for words. Miss Lyon was also surprised, but her astonishment expressed itself in a torrent of conversation.

"Do you really admire them, Miss Taylor?" Rebecca gushed. "It would be my pleasure to teach you how to paint, if you are sincere in your admiration, and perhaps you, in return, could teach me how to sew. I am frightfully backward in the art, which causes my mother immense pain."

"If the arrangement meets the approval of Mrs Lyon, I should be very happy to do so," replied Miss Taylor.

Mrs Lyon shot a hasty glance in Hannah's direction, but Hannah's downcast eyes were busy examining the remains of a piece of seed cake that sat on her plate.

"I fear this is an unfair bargain," said Mrs Lyon. "You are an accomplished needlewoman, Miss Taylor, while my daughter is still learning her craft."

"Her lively conversation shall right the imbalance," replied Miss Taylor. "The afternoons are often long, and I would be glad of the company."

The matter was therefore settled to the mutual satisfaction of Miss Taylor and Rebecca, and not long afterward Miss Taylor took her leave. Rebecca, expecting to hear praises for the brilliant way in which she had secured Miss Taylor for a sewing instructress, was dismayed to find herself berated from practically all sides.

"What did I do wrong?" she pleaded, turning from the black looks emanating from her mother to the more benign, but still disappointed frown that had appeared on Hannah's face.

"The plan was to provide Miss Taylor with a more practical remuneration," Hannah said softly.

"She needs money, not painting lessons," Mrs Lyon explained in her usual forthright manner. "You have ruined everything, with your interfering."

"The child meant well," said Mrs Baer, giving Rebecca's arm a reassuring pat. "And, Rebecca, you managed to openly reveal the amiable heart that I could only suspect that Miss Taylor possesses. Her praises of your china plates and desire to become further acquainted with you, despite the difference in your ages, are ample proof that she is as eager to please others as she is to be pleased by her new friends. It is a great advantage in life to be happy with whatever circumstances the Al-Mighty has placed you in, which is why I think that Miss Taylor and Mr Jacob Oppenheim will be very happy together."

"Mr Oppenheim? Why, of course!" Mrs Lyon exclaimed. "Hannah, you remember Mr Oppenheim, do you not?"

The pinkish tint that appeared on Hannah's cheeks made words unnecessary. How could anyone in the Lyon family forget the great service that Mr Oppenheim, a former assistant in Mr Lyon's fashionable clockmaker's shop, had done for Mr Lyon, when that gentleman was faced with financial ruin? Or that Mr Oppenheim had harboured a secret hope that he might one day ask for Hannah's hand in marriage—a hope that was dashed when Hannah married Mr David Goldsmith, instead? Since the matrimonial alliance between Hannah and Mr Goldsmith had been approved by Mrs Baer, there was no doubt that this was truly a match made in heaven. But even while the Jewish community was dancing at Hannah's wedding, there was one unresolved matter that had cast a slight twinge of sadness upon the otherwise joyous occasion—when would Mr Oppenheim also attain such happiness and find his intended bride?

"But Mr Oppenheim now lives in Manchester," said Hannah, her composure completely regained. "How shall you arrange a meeting between him and Miss Taylor?"

"Oh, I will think of something," replied Mrs Baer, her eyes twinkling with pleasure. "Manchester is not on the other side of the sea. Boney shall not prevent this marriage from taking place, if it is meant to be."

"Mr Oppenheim and Miss Taylor," Mrs Lyon murmured happily, apparently already seeing, in her mind's eye, the happy couple standing under the marriage canopy. "It is a brilliant suggestion, Mrs

Baer, but are you sure Mr Oppenheim will not mind that his bride has no dowry?"

"No dowry?" The light departed from Mrs Baer's eyes. "Are you sure?"

"Mr Lyon has heard that Miss Taylor and her brother are practically penniless."

"That does complicate matters. If it is not Boney, it is something else," said Mrs Baer with a sigh. "No wonder our Sages say that finding a marriage partner is as difficult as splitting the sea."

At this second mention of "Boney," the English patriot's name for the Frenchman who has wrecked such havoc in these times, Napoleon Bonaparte, the talk turned to news about the war and the battle that had recently taken place near a Portuguese village called Fuentes de Onoro. While Mrs Lyon lamented the fact that the Portuguese and Spanish would insist on calling their villages and towns by the most fantastic and unpronounceable names, Mrs Baer expressed an opinion that Viscount Wellington was stretching his troops too thin. Or so Mr Baer had said, and he was in a position to know since his coffee house—a kosher establishment situated in the City—was frequented by some who were privy to information not readily available to the general public.

"They say that more than a thousand of our troops were killed," said Mrs Baer, "and that the French losses were twice as many, if not more. I do not see why Boney cannot be content with being the Emperor of the French. Why must he insist on ruling the entire world?"

While the married ladies discussed this interesting question, Rebecca had other weighty matters to consider. Somehow, she must repair the damage she had caused to the Taylors and think of a way to transfer payment for her sewing lessons into Miss Taylor's hand without causing the young lady embarrassment. As her brain was unusually devoid of ideas, she decided to ask the opinion of Miss Harriet Franks.

Ever since the Franks family had returned to Devonshire Square — a happy event that had occurred after Mr Franks had been cleared of the charge of being a spy for Napoleon — the two young ladies had resumed their friendship as though there had never been a separation. Thus, Perl, the Lyon family's housemaid, was not surprised to see Rebecca slip on a pelisse over her muslin dress and then dash out the front door. Nor was the housemaid of the Franks family surprised to see Miss Lyon standing on the doorstep of the Franks's residence, which was only two doors down from Rebecca's home. During the course of almost any day there were any number of reasons why two young ladies of not quite the marriageable age must consult one another for sage advice and judicious opinion. On this occasion, though, Rebecca was very surprised to be informed that she could not see her friend.

"Miss Franks is indisposed," said the housemaid. "The entire family is indisposed."

Rebecca noticed at once the girl's anxious expression. "It is not serious, I hope."

"I am sure I do not know, Miss. Perhaps Mr Taylor can tell you, for I think I hear him coming down the stairs now."

The housemaid opened the front door wider, so that Rebecca could see inside. Mr Taylor was, indeed, descending the stairs. Yet unlike the sweeping wooden staircase, which had been polished until the steps shone like new, the young physician looked curiously worn and troubled.

"Mr Taylor, perhaps you will remember me. I am Rebecca Lyon. You and Miss Taylor were at my family's Seder."

Mr Taylor bowed, in acknowledgement of her salutation. "I hope no one in your family has taken ill, Miss Lyon."

"No, thank G-d. But Miss Franks is my very best friend in the entire world. Please say that I may see her, and that her condition is not serious. And that her parents will recover, as well."

For the first time, Mr Taylor smiled. "I apologize that my gloomy expression has needlessly alarmed you. I have every expectation that your friend and Mr and Mrs Franks will recover. I believe it is nothing more than an indisposition brought on by a tainted piece of fish. But because they have all spent an uncomfortable night, I think it best that they spend today resting undisturbed. If, however, you would like to send a note to Miss Franks, I am sure it will do her much good."

"You have relieved my mind immensely," Rebecca replied.

The housemaid allowed Rebecca to enter the drawing room, where Rebecca knew that paper and pen and ink would be at her disposal. While she wrote her note, Mr Taylor requested that the housemaid escort him to the kitchen so that he could give instructions to the cook.

Dear Harriet (she wrote),

Your illness has alarmed me to no end, and I should have been frantic with worry had not Mr Taylor assured me that you will soon be well. Please follow his instructions diligently, as I have a very important matter to discuss with you. I will fly to your bedside as soon as I hear that you are strong enough to receive a visitor.

Your faithful friend who intends not to sleep a wink until she hears that Hashem has sent you a complete recovery,

Rebecca

P.S. Isaac tried to say my name today. I am sure of it. But that is not the matter I wish to discuss with you.

P.P.S. Please send my compliments to Mr and Mrs Franks and my best wishes for their speedy and complete recovery.

When she was quite sure that she had no more postscripts to add to her letter, she carefully blotted the page and waited for the ink to dry. By the time she was ready to hand the important missive to the Franks's housemaid, Mr Taylor was also ready to depart.

"May I walk you to your door, Miss Lyon?"

Rebecca was momentarily flustered. She had never walked alone with a man who was not a member of her family — unless it was with their servant Meshullam Mendel, who was almost like a family member — and even though the distance was just a few steps away she was not sure if she should accept the invitation or find a reason to remain in the Franks's home. But Mr Taylor was already leading her to the pavement, and in an instant he made his intentions clear.

"I did not wish to speak in front of the servants," he said, "but I am curious about one thing. Is their cook newly employed, or has she been with the Franks family for some time?"

"Oh, she has been their cook forever - or at least for as long as I can remember."

"Thank you. Good evening."

They had reached Rebecca's home at the same moment that Mr Lyon was returning from his shop on Cornhill Street. Mr Lyon raised an eyebrow, but before he could say a word his daughter told him the distressing news concerning the Franks family.

"Is there anything we can do?" he asked Mr Taylor. "Perhaps we can send over some soup?"

"I have spoken with their cook and she has assured me that she has everything she needs to prepare the family's meals according to my instructions. Good evening, Mr Lyon." Mr Taylor then bowed again to Rebecca and said, "Good evening, Miss Lyon. I hope that tomorrow will bring you happier tidings concerning your friend."

Mr Taylor turned to go, but Mr Lyon called after him, "Mr Taylor, will you not join us for supper? We would be honoured if you would dine with us."

"Thank you, but my sister is waiting for me in our rooms."

The young man bowed again, and hurried out of the square.

CHAPTER III

When Mr Taylor returned to his rooms, his sister was waiting for him, as he had said. However, there was another person in the room, as well.

"Good evening, sir," said the stranger. "I see by your expression that you do not know me, but I trust that we will soon be happy to have made one another's acquaintance."

Here the merchant—for it was all too evident from the man's familiar ways that he was one of those who are friends with the world not because he cherishes friendship for itself but because he sees in the world a herd of potential buyers for his wares—showed the object he was holding in his hand, a metal tin.

"Yesterday, tea was the exclusive pleasure of the English aristocrat," the merchant babbled on, "a beverage drunk only in the highest circles. Today all that is changed, thanks to the enterprise I am proud to represent: Amos & Amos. Remember the name, sir, for the next time you will be coming to me, and not I to you. It is our privilege to have found a way to make this drink of the gods affordable to those who inhabit less lofty spheres. And I was just remarking to your wife, who cannot hide her expertise in the housewifely arts from an eye as skilled as mine, she will find no better quality tea for so reasonable a price anywhere else in London. How many tins would you like to purchase, sir? I usually am allowed to sell only one sample tin to a household, but because I see that you are a man of some intelligence and refinement I will make an exemption and sell you two."

The merchant had already set down upon the table the tin he had been holding in his hand and was about to reach into his great coat's pocket for the promised second tin, when Mr Taylor stopped him. "You need not trouble yourself, Mr ..."

"Amos, sir. My brother, Mr Lazer Amos, is the genius behind our manufacturing process, while I, Baruch Amos, am merely his humble representative in the marketplace."

"We do not drink tea, Mr Amos. Good evening."

"That is my point exactly, sir," replied Mr Amos, refusing to be so easily rebuffed. "Why should not respectable working people such as yourself and your Missus be able to drink a refreshing cup of tea at the end of a long and tiring day? Why should tea leaves, which grow in such abundance in G-d's glorious world, be priced so high in the desultory world devised by mortal man? These are the sorts of questions my brother and I asked one another. This is the answer."

Two tins of tea were now sitting on the table. Mr Taylor could see that his sister—he had not bothered to correct the merchant's mistake—was looking at the tins with a longing eye. But he remained resolute. Returning the tins to the merchant's hands, he said, "I shall not repeat myself a third time, sir. We do not drink tea."

Mr Amos received the rejected tins with solemn dignity, and bowed his way to the door. But before he departed in defeat, he shot off one last salvo into the fray. "Amos & Amos. Mark my words, one day you will be coming to me, sir, and not I to you."

The door closed. Mr Taylor gave a weary sigh of relief as he sank down onto a chair. "Why did you let him come inside, Elisheva?"

"It has been so long since we have had tea with our supper. And he said the tea he was offering was so reasonable. And ..." Her voice drifted off into silence.

"And you hate having to live in poverty, watching every penny, not being able to afford a new dress or pay social calls to the other young ladies in the neighbourhood, such as Mrs Hannah Goldsmith."

"You are not being fair, Gabriel. I have never complained about helping you advance in your career. But you, at least, are out in the world. You see people. You converse with them. I remain inside these four walls every day."

Mr Taylor loosened the stiff cravat wound about his neck, and as the linen folds gave way his stern expression softened, as well. "I apologize. I should not have spoken so harshly to you. But, Elisheva, if I ask you to economize, I ask it for your own good. If you are to marry, you will need a dowry. The few pennies saved on a tin of tea may not seem much in and of themselves, but over time the money saved will accumulate."

"When? When I am an old woman ready for the grave?"

Elisheva Taylor was not a young lady who often allowed herself the luxury of a good cry, but the deprivations endured during the last several years had accumulated to such an extent that the barriers she had erected between her sense of duty and her natural sensibilities now tore apart and a torrent of tears ushered forth. Her brother waited patiently for the storm to subside, and then gently asked, "I know it is not the tea you are weeping over, Elisheva. What has happened? What has changed?"

The young lady wiped away the few remaining tears with the corner of her apron and said, "I was invited to the home of Mrs Lyon, to Devonshire Square."

"For what reason?"

"I am not sure I know. The ladies were all doing some sewing. We talked. We had cakes, and tea."

"It was pleasant?"

"Yes, it was pleasant to be in company again. But when I returned home, and it was all so silent …"

"Mrs Goldsmith was there, with her child?"

Elisheva did not reply.

"I promise you, Elisheva," said Mr Taylor, rising from his chair to place his hands on his younger sister's shoulders, "that one day you shall also be a happily married woman, surrounded by your children. And it shall be when you are still young. It shall be soon."

They were interrupted by a knock at the door.

"If it is Amos & Amos calling again, I shall …" Mr Taylor opened the door, but he had no need to complete his threat. The tea merchant must have gone to find greener fields, for he was not the one standing at the door.

"Alt clo's, sir?" asked an elderly Jew, dressed in ragged clothes, whose hoary head was crowned by a faded, low-sitting, flat-brimmed hat, which had been the height of fashion some ten years previously and from which there now escaped several tangled strands of white hair in a straggly fashion. "Buy or sell, I am at your service, sir."

"Come in and I shall ask my sister."

The old man, whose name was Jeremiah Schneider, entered the room and Mr Taylor quickly closed the door. "Have a seat, sir," he said to the elderly Jew. "Elisheva, is there still some salop?"

The old clothes man sat down, while Elisheva went to the hearth and removed the kettle from the hob. She poured some of the hot water into two mugs, and then into each added a spoonful of powdered orchid root. When the powder had dissolved, she added a few drops of rosewater, to sweeten the brew.

"Will you not join us, Elisheva?" asked the old man, after Elisheva had placed the two mugs on the table.

"I am not thirsty," she replied.

"She was invited to take tea at Devonshire Square," Mr Taylor added.

The elderly Jew raised his bushy white eyebrows. "Devonshire Square? That's a fine place to wet your whistle. So is Bury Street, for that matter. But I have not come to pay a social call. I am in trouble, Gabriel."

"What kind of trouble?"

"Hanging trouble."

* * *

"Search, sir, at your leisure. My abode is at your disposal."

The Earl of Gravel Lane returned his attention to the dirt-caked fragment of mirror that stood upon the mantelpiece and reviewed his toilette. Fortunately, the room was dimly lit and so he did not have to see the reason why his powdered wig had been discarded in the dust bin several years before by its former owner, who most likely had found it in another dust bin, where it had been discarded by the owner before him. When the Earl looked into his mirror, he saw only what he wished to see. And at that particular moment the young Jewish man who had dubbed himself a peer of the realm at a time when most of England's Jews were barred from being citizens of their adopted land had no wish to see the angry visage of the Bow Street Runner, who was looking about the Earl's broken-down kingdom with a look of anger tempered with extreme distaste.

"Tell me where you've stashed the stolen clothes, Earl, and I'll put in a word with the magistrate to have your sentence reduced from hanging to transportation."

The Earl turned and put his quizzing glass to his eye. "I have no wish to travel to Australia, and heaven can wait."

The Bow Street Runner scowled. This was not the first time he had paid the Earl a call, and never once had he succeeded in bringing the young man to justice, a circumstance that irked him to no end. "You won't wiggle out of it this time. I have a witness who saw some of your boys break into that house last night."

"Which ear does your witness see from?"

The Bow Street Runner did not deign to reply. Instead, he ordered his two assistants to search the room, a task that was quickly accomplished since there was very little in the room to search. The Earl possessed only one threadbare suit of clothes, as did the other boys that comprised his circle, and so there was no need for cupboards and chests to store belongings which none of them possessed.

"Go search the other rooms," growled the Runner.

"Without a candle, sir?" asked one of the assistants.

"Take mine," said the Earl, offering, with a magnanimous gesture, the lopsided candelabra where only one candle was lit. "I am not afraid of the dark."

Again the Bow Street Runner did not rise to take the bait. The truth was that he knew that if the Earl had been involved in the break-in at Wentworth Street, the stolen goods would have already been sold to someone else. The only hope he had of cracking the case was to bully some of the Earl's boys into a confession. But the Earl's rooms on Gravel Lane were curiously silent.

"My companions are taking an evening stroll," said the Earl, sensing in which direction the Runner's thoughts were going. "It would be a shame to not take advantage of such lovely spring weather."

"You never seem to take much exercise."

"Gout," replied the Earl, with a shrug that suggested both the pain of his affliction and his stoic refusal to pay that pain any notice.

The Bow Street Runner might have inquired how a skinny young man who had been a street urchin almost since birth could have become afflicted with a wealthy man's disease, but he did not bother. He was not interested in the Earl's affectations.

"Think over my offer, Earl. One of the handkerchiefs was marked, although the initials were so small you might not have seen them, especially in this dim light. And my witness is a sharp lad with two good eyes. Good-night."

The Runner and his assistants left the room. A few moments later the front door to the building was heard to slam shut. That signal having been heard, one of the decaying wooden panels in the room was pushed open and General Well'ngone, the Earl's right-hand man, slipped out of his hiding place and into the room.

"It sounds like someone has got it in for us," said General Well'ngone. "Our boys weren't anywhere near Wentworth last night."

"It was Smalley who sold us those clothes, wasn't it?"

"Do you think Smalley has turned active citizen?"

"It wouldn't be the first time."

General Well'ngone, whose youth was accentuated by his oversized military great coat, which he wore year round, no matter the weather, pushed his bicorne hat to the back of his head and gave a low whistle. "But the Runners won't be able to lay their hands on us, unless they've traced the handkerchief to old Jeremiah, and he wouldn't tattle on us for fiddler's money. Would he?"

CHAPTER IV

Mr Ezra Melamed was engaged in a game of chess with his friend and business partner, Mr Arthur Powell, the younger son of Lord James Powell, when the Bow Street Runner requested an interview. Mr Melamed instructed his butler to admit the man of law and order, while Mr Powell, aware that something of an embarrassing nature concerning London's Jewish community was most likely going to be discussed, discretely removed himself to the map table.

The Bow Street Runner took note of Mr Melamed's elegant apartment, as well as the nobleman's son ensconced by the window, and arranged his speech accordingly. "With all due respect, Mr Melamed, the people of London have had just about enough. Between your young Jewish ruffians and your old clothes men, there won't be a shirt left on the honest backs of a single English workingman."

Mr Melamed motioned for the Runner to sit down and offered him a glass of wine, which was accepted. Then the benefactor of London's Jewish community, who often acted as the liaison between the community and the Crown, requested to be informed of what had happened this time.

"Three shirts, two nightcaps, and a handkerchief were removed from the premises belonging to a tanner named John Whittlecupper the night before last, while the tanner and his wife were sleeping in their beds. I have a witness who says the thieves were some of the Earl of Gravel Lane's boys."

"Have you arrested them?" asked Mr Melamed.

"Not yet." The Runner replaced his wine goblet on the table and casually lay his right hand on the table beside it, palm up.

"Why not?" asked Mr Melamed, ignoring the upturned hand and its hint that all could be amicably resolved with a generous bribe. "I can assure you that I am no friend of the Earl, whom I consider to be a corrupter of Jewish youth and, as you say, a menace to the honest people of London. The Crown may transport him to Australia with my blessing."

Mr Melamed rose from his chair and said, "Good-day, sir." However, the Bow Street Runner would not be so quickly dismissed.

"There is a problem, Mr Melamed. My witness, a good man in many respects, was not completely sober on the night in question. Therefore, he did not get as clear a look at the thieves as a court of law might wish."

"So you have no real proof that the Earl and his boys were involved?"

"Not in the breaking in, but we do have proof that the stolen goods ended up in the Earl's hands."

"And what proof is that?"

"I have a witness who saw one of the Earl's boys sell the goods to an old clothes man named Jeremiah Schneider. I don't know what happened to the rest of the things, but the handkerchief, which was embroidered with the initials J. W., was found in Jeremiah's pile of old clothes this afternoon."

"Have you arrested Mr Schneider?"

"Not yet. He slipped through a trap door hidden behind a curtain, while we were examining his wares. But when I do find him, the old man won't escape from me a second time. I promise."

"Mr Schneider is an elderly man?"

"If his white hairs aren't lying, I'd guess he remembers pretty well the coronation of our old, mad King George, may the good Lord restore him to good health. I, myself, don't like to arrest an old man, knowing as I do that he won't have the strength to survive the sentence of penal servitude that a court of law is sure to impose. But what can I do, sir? Duty is duty and I must serve the Crown, whether that crown rests upon the head of a loony or a man as sane as me or you."

Mr Melamed was silent. He was very aware that some one hundred and fifty years ago his ancestors had arrived in London as penniless refugees, and that it was thanks to the One Above that their efforts to establish themselves in their adopted home had been crowned with success. Such success had not been granted to every member of the Jewish community who had come afterward. Thus, there were many Jewish orphans who roamed the streets of London and grabbed whatever they could to stay alive, whether it was an honest day's work or a stolen handkerchief. The old clothes men, who were often as old and worn out with care as the rags they peddled, caused problems of a different kind. Much of their merchandise was, indeed, cast off clothing that had been obtained lawfully. However, they were not above purchasing stolen goods, which they resold for a few pennies more than they had paid. Mr Melamed would have preferred to keep a distance from these unsavoury characters, but it was impossible. A theft perpetrated by a Jewish ruffian cast a slur upon the reputation of every Jew in London.

If he could have set up each poor Jew in a self-supporting business endeavour, he would have done so. But even though he was an extremely wealthy man he did not possess wealth enough to accomplish that lofty goal. And so he was in a bind, a most uncomfortable bind. If he left the riffraff to their fate, his heart would berate his intellect for being cruel. But if he bailed out each miscreant what would he achieve? The person would only return to the same disreputable streets and thieve again—and the Bow Street Runners and Magistrates would grumble about the Jews, who were all thick as thieves in their opinion, conveniently forgetting their own underhanded business of taking bribes. Yes, it was a nasty puzzle, and Mr Melamed was momentarily irritated with the world that had placed the puzzle at his door.

However, he was saved from having to make an answer by Mr Powell, who had grown restless and had now approached the man from Bow Street.

"Did I hear you say that Mr Schneider is an elderly gentleman?"

"Yes, sir."

"My father gave some clothes to an old Jew the other day. Are you quite sure that the initials on that handkerchief were J. W., and not J. W. P., the initials of my father, Lord James Walmsley Powell?" asked

Mr Powell, slipping a few coins into the Runner's coat pocket.

"I see what you mean, sir. Most likely there has been a mistake and I thank you for clearing it up in such a handsome manner. I will pass along the word that Mr Schneider need no longer fear arrest." The Runner bowed to Mr Powell. He then turned to Mr Melamed and said, "I am sorry to have troubled you, Mr Melamed. Good-day."

When the Bow Street Runner had left the room, Mr Melamed said, "Powell, you did not have to do that."

"No, but I was not about to allow our game to be disrupted by a trifle." Mr Powell raised an ebony chess piece and placed it on the board. "Checkmate."

***

Mr Powell left Bury Street in excellent spirits; he had dined well, despite his host's strict adherence to the ancient laws of maintaining a kosher diet; he had won at chess; and he had convinced Mr Melamed to invest in the building of a new neighbourhood to be located on the north-western outskirts of London.

Although Mr Powell had been born into the gentry, his tardy entrance into that society — he was a younger son — had precluded him from inheriting his family's wealth. He therefore had been forced to make his own way in the world. After a bad wound in the leg put an end to his distinguished army career, he returned to London determined to distinguish himself in some other way. Some rash business decisions almost landed him on Queer Street, but marriage to a young heiress had saved him from the ignominious fate of bankruptcy. That marriage had been happy but brief, and when his wife died in childbirth the fortune she had brought to the marriage devolved, due to a curious clause in her grandfather's will, to a male cousin.

Once again Mr Powell was left to his own devices, only this time he was not alone: he had a son, Thomas, to provide for. It was at this time that he entered into a business partnership with Mr Melamed, who had distinguished himself as a shrewd investor in London's rapidly expanding real estate market, as had his father and grandfather before him.

Indeed, the Melamed and Powell families were first brought together after the Great Fire of London in 1666, when the city was in the midst of rebuilding its charred places of business and homes. The Mr Melamed of that generation, who was a new immigrant to England but wise in the ways of property, supplied the knowledge, while the Stuart-era Mr Powell supplied the capital and the social position needed to smooth the way for the young Jew's path.

With time, the fortunes of the Melamed family increased, while their reputation for being honest brokers became firmly and widely established. Yet even though they no longer needed the services of the Powell family, the younger generation was instructed to remember the kindness that had been done for them in earlier years. Therefore, when the benighted financial position of the Mr Powell of our present story was brought to the attention of Mr Ezra Melamed, the man of business hastened to assist the young gentleman by making Mr Powell a partner in a new endeavour. Since Mr Powell showed a good aptitude for the business of buying and selling property, the partnership continued, eventually attaining that happy state where the two men approached their mutual business concerns as equal partners, trusted advisors, and valued friends.

But none of this was on Mr Powell's mind as he alighted from his carriage, which had come to a halt at a Mayfair establishment owned by his cousin by marriage, Lady Marblehead. Mr Powell noted with satisfaction that the steps leading up to the freshly painted door were swept clean and the brass doorknocker shaped in the head of a lion gleamed; apparently Lady Marblehead's steps to economize, a regime that had been put into place after the death of her husband, had not yet been extended to the facade of her home. The true state of the Marblehead fortune was therefore still a question mark. Had Lord Marblehead truly squandered the fortune of Mr Powell's deceased wife? Or had Lady Marblehead decided upon her own advice that she was on the brink of poverty and disgrace, as widows sometimes did? Powell did not know, but he certainly hoped that Lady Marblehead's recent economies were due to an elderly woman's eccentricity and not to an elderly Lord's mismanagement of his financial affairs.

Whatever the true reason, unused rooms now saw their furniture shrouded and their doors locked, while the smallest possible fires were lit in the rooms that were still used. The carriage and the coachman were discharged from service, as were one of the two parlour maids and the cook's assistant. In accordance with the changes in the diet of the mistress of the house, the generous tea service that had served the

Marblehead family for more than eighty years was replaced with a new one comprised of teacups so dainty that only two swallows of tea could be poured into them. The plates for serving cakes were of a similar diminutive size. Therefore, any man with a reasonably hearty appetite would be well advised to sup at home or at his club before taking tea with Lady Marblehead.

Because he had supped well, Mr Powell was prepared to be satisfied with the little that was offered to him in the way of refreshments, just as he was prepared to listen politely to the seemingly endless supply of ailments that his elderly cousin was forced to suffer − although he was certain that the only ailment that Lady Marblehead truly suffered from was boredom. Lady Marblehead, who was childless, had hinted, more than once, that whatever little she did possess would most likely be inherited by Mr Powell's son. Ordinarily, it would be the son's place to humour his future benefactress. But since the young man was fighting with Viscount Wellington's troops in Portugal, the task had fallen to the boy's father, Mr Powell.

Meanwhile, Lady Marblehead showed no signs of departing for that better world, despite her many protestations that this world offered nothing but pain and grief. Indeed, when Mr Powell entered the drawing room, the elderly lady was engaged in a most lively conversation with a man many years her junior.

"Ah, Powell, there you are. You are a former army man. You shall be the judge of this argument between us. You remember, my sister's grandson … no, I suppose you do not. His parents moved to

Jamaica before you were married. Mr Arthur Powell, Mr William Clyde."

The two men bowed. Mr Clyde retook his seat next to Lady Marblehead, while Mr Powell found a seat opposite. While Lady Marblehead poured out the requisite two swallows-full of tea into Mr Powell's cup, she said, with a voice that was remarkably strong and shrill, "One of us insists that Viscount Wellington is making a muddle of the Peninsular Campaign. One thousand lives lost in three days, or so they say. What do you think, Powell?"

Mr Powell, who had served with Viscount Wellington in India, disliked it when civilians who knew nothing of army life and the challenges of the battlefield openly and contemptuously expressed their painfully unknowledgeable opinions about the war with the French. If such a comment had been made in his club, he would have made a swift retort and silenced the speaker. But as he warily eyed the young man sitting opposite him, who was gazing back at him with an air of smug satisfaction, Mr Powell was overcome with an uncomfortable feeling that a trap had been laid in the room — and he was the one who was going to be caught in its steel teeth.

Who had spoken for Viscount Wellington and who had spoken against him? Mr Powell looked from one face to another, but neither Lady Marblehead nor Mr Clyde gave him a hint as to what lay behind their smiling facades. What Mr Powell did know was that Lady Marblehead never liked to be openly contradicted, and so he said, "I am no longer privy to army secrets, and so I am unable to enlighten you as to the true state of affairs in Spain and Portugal. But I can say that it is commendable of you both to be concerned about our troops; so few people care about the plight of the common soldier."

"I care nothing for the common soldier," replied Lady Marblehead. "I care only that your fool of a son does not land on the wrong end of a French bayonet before this wasteful war is over. That is why I say that Wellington must be replaced."

"I thank you, ma'am, for your concern. I am confident that the boy will do all in his power to return to England alive."

"Your son is in Portugal, Mr Powell?" asked Mr Clyde.

"He is."

"I should like to enlist. But when I received word that my dear aunt was in ill health, I felt it was my duty to be here, instead."

Mr Powell's raised an eyebrow; if there had been a change in Lady Marblehead's health, it was a surprise to him. But Lady Marblehead, upon hearing those words, leaned back in her chair and let escape from her thin lips a mournful sigh.

"Are you not well, ma'am?" asked Mr Clyde with alarm. "Shall I send for your physician?"
The elderly woman waved her handkerchief, a gesture with which Mr Powell was familiar from previous visits. He settled back into his chair, making himself comfortable for the speech he knew would follow. In contrast, Mr Clyde, who had only recently arrived upon the scene and therefore was unfamiliar with his great-aunt's histrionics, stood up in readiness to fly, if necessary.

"What good can physicians and their medicines do for me now? I am an old woman. It is time I cast off this mortal coil and give up my place to another." Lady Marblehead paused to see what sort of affect her words were having. A slight smile played about her lips, as she said, "Do sit down and have some more tea, Clyde. I am not going to die today."

The drowsy, drooping eyes of Mr Powell shot open. Lady Marblehead never offered her guests a second cup of tea.

"I have not lost my senses, cousin," said Lady Marblehead, still smiling the same smile as she gazed in Mr Powell's direction.

"The thought did not occur to me, ma'am."

"I have a new physician, a Jew. Perhaps your friend Mr Melamed knows him. His name is Taylor. Gabriel Taylor."

"I do not recall hearing the name. You are satisfied with his treatments?"

"I find the young man amusing. He insists that I could live to be a hundred, if I would change my habits. Instead of my usual supper of bread and butter and weak tea, he says I must eat meat and drink a glass of wine. I must also partake of a full tea in the afternoon. He even suggested I should take a drive in the park every day, for the fresh air. I assured him that the drive, at least, would do me no good. True elegance has departed from the world, and I cannot abide to see it replaced by mere puppets of fashion. But I did say I would try to force myself to eat a few more mouthfuls, if he insisted. Have another piece of sponge cake, Powell."

"And has your health improved?" asked Mr Powell, selecting a piece of cake from the silver platter that had been shoved in his direction.

"He charges half the fee that Mr Crawley charged me, which has already done my heart much good. Perhaps I shall live to one hundred. That would surprise some people."

Lady Marblehead laughed, but she was the only one in the room who did.

CHAPTER V

Mr Clyde had already dressed for dinner and was sipping a glass of sherry in the library when he heard the front bell ring. A few moments later he heard the door open and the sound of voices in the vestibule. Perhaps in some other home he would not have been interested to know who was at the front door and what their business was, but in this instance he was very interested, since it concerned Lady Marblehead's affairs.

He would have been highly surprised if anyone should look upon this lively interest with suspicion. Indeed, he liked to think of himself as being a remarkably frank and open young man. He would have told anyone that under the terms of Lady Marblehead's present will he did not expect to inherit much; for some reason the old woman had not been as fond of her great-nephew as said great-nephew could have wished. But now that she was practically at death's door, he intended to raise himself in her affection and esteem — and thereby raise the amount of his inheritance in the new will that he hoped he would be able to convince Lady Marblehead to write. All of this was something that any young man in his position would attempt, he assured himself. To sit back and do nothing to improve his circumstances would have shown a lack of spirit.

By standing just inside the partially open door, he could hear that the visitor was being ushered into the drawing room. Then he heard the sound of the servant's footsteps retreating down the hallway. What could be more natural than for Mr Clyde to drift into the drawing room, where he would naturally expect to see Lady Marblehead? And if he should see the visitor instead, well, who could object to that?

The manoeuvre was accomplished. The visitor turned when Mr Clyde entered the room.

"Oh, it is you," said Mr Clyde.

* * *

Mr Powell was seated in his accustomed seat at White's, his gentlemen's club, but unusually out of temper. The afternoon, which had begun with so much promise, had taken a fall and his spirits had tumbled with it. After his visit to Lady Marblehead he had returned home to dress for dinner, and it was then that he was informed that an urgent letter from his son was waiting for his immediate response. Although Mr Powell had just the one son, he had many acquaintances and so he knew what such a letter meant, even before he took up his pen knife and broke open the seal.

As Mr Powell had expected, his son had written because of his gambling debts. Young men, especially young officers who had nothing better to do in the evening than play cards with their fellow officers, often got into financial trouble in this way. What followed, though, had not been expected. If his son could not repay those debts of honour very soon, the young man had written, he would be cashiered, given a dishonourable discharge from the army.

Mr Powell had read those words with a potent mixture of alarm and anger. Such a thing had never happened before in the Powell family, whose distinguished service on the battlefield could be traced back as far as the Battle of Bosworth, that famous battle which signalled the end of the War of the Roses and the beginning of the Tudor dynasty. He had therefore rushed through the ensuing torrent of words—his son's apologies and pleas for financial assistance—to reach the named sum that would restore honour to the Powell name. The amount had made him gasp.

And so Mr Powell sat gloomily in his club, his face buried behind his newspaper, which he barely noticed. He would have to raise the money somehow, but how? He could sell some of his properties in London; indeed, he knew exactly which ones he wanted to sell. But he had intended to use the proceeds from the sale to finance the building of a new London neighbourhood—a transaction which would increase the family's prosperity and not deplete it, as would paying off his son's debts of honour. There was a rare, old set of sapphire and diamond jewellery that he could sell, but it had been in the family for generations and, again, he hated the thought of depleting the family jewellery box for such a reason. Then his thoughts turned, without his quite noticing how, to the locked cupboards that could be found in Lady Marblehead's Mayfair residence.

Although he certainly wished his cousin no harm, the thought of that heavy, old silver tea service locked away, doing no one any good, as well as the jewellery box that was gathering dust in the lady's dressing table drawer, made him recall with exceptional ill humour the memory of Lady Marblehead's words, that she might live for another thirty years or more. Of course, Mr Powell might have asked his cousin for a loan, since the old woman had a soft spot for Thomas and had excused the boy's scrapes before. But the arrival of Mr Clyde at precisely this moment was awkward. The sum that Mr Powell needed was not a trifling one. What if Mr Clyde took advantage of Thomas's excesses at the gaming table and used it to turn Lady Marblehead's affections toward him instead?

A loud peal of thunder further jarred Mr Powell's unsettled nerves, as well as interrupted the irreverent patter of a noisy party of young dandies seated in the club's bow window.

"I bet you £500 there is a second peal of thunder before I count to fifty," said Lord Alvanley, who was on leave from his regiment and bored as only a wealthy young gentleman can be.

His companion accepted the bet, which was duly entered into the club's book.

"Anyone else?" Lord Alvanley looked about the crowded room. A few other young men entered their wagers. However, when Lord Alvanley's jovial eye fell upon Mr Powell, the older man said, with barely concealed disgust, "I would just as soon bet upon which raindrop will reach the bottom of the window pane first."

* * *

When the storm broke it found Miss Elisheva Taylor hurrying down a crowded street, with only a straw bonnet and a thin pelisse to protect her from the raindrops that pelted the passers-by and quickly formed fast-moving streams and puddles in the roads. She was further distressed when a carriage came hurtling down the street, splattering her clothing from head to toe. She watched it go on its way — its passengers not caring about the damage they had done — with rising anger.

She did not like London — the crowds, the dirt, the dismal weather. But what could she do? Where could she go? Her brother had no wish to return to Jamaica, and she could not return there alone. But on a day like this, she longed for the warmth of the hot Jamaican sun. For a moment she closed her eyes, for even the thought of it was so comforting and enticing.

A second splatter made her open her eyes with a start. This time, though, the vehicle did not travel on. A man jumped down from it and said with alarm, "I beg your pardon, madam. Would you …" the man stopped and studied Miss Taylor's face. "We have met before, madam, I am sure of it. Amos is my name, Baruch Amos of Amos & Amos fame. I will never forgive myself for causing a fellow person this inconvenience, not to mention the possibility of your catching your death of cold. May my carriage take you to your home? May I do you this service?"

Ordinarily Miss Taylor would not have accepted the invitation. But she saw that also inside the carriage was a young boy of about seven or eight, and so she felt that she would not exceed the bounds of propriety if she did accept, especially since she was feeling rather chilled after the two splatterings of her clothes. However, instead of asking to be taken to Bury Street, she said that she wished to be taken to the Jewish orphanage, where she sometimes volunteered her services by helping with the sewing and mending, or by giving the children their supper.

"I shall be able to dry my coat there," she explained, when Mr Amos protested that she must consider her own health first.

When they reached the orphanage, Mr Amos insisted that she accept from him a small present, by which he would know that her forgiveness was complete. "This package contains five tins of tea, madam, which some connoisseurs consider to be the best tea in the world. Even those who cannot appreciate this blend of tea's exquisite taste will appreciate its attractive price. Serve it to those poor orphaned children, if you prefer not to accept the gift for yourself, for I see that you are a selfless person who is always thinking of others. I ask only that you remember the name—Amos & Amos—and that you give the tea with my compliments to the housekeeper of this venerable institution."

Mrs Halberstein, who was in charge of the orphanage's kitchen, made a fuss over Miss Taylor the instant that the young woman entered the room, where, fortunately, a large fire was burning in the hearth.

"I have made a nice soup for the children's supper," she told Miss Taylor. "I shall bring you a bowl now."

A grateful Elisheva did not protest. If she could not have sunshine, a warm fire would do. The motherly fussing of Mrs Halberstein, who was a childless widow, was also welcome. And as she sipped the hot soup, and recalled the kindness of the tea merchant, she thought that perhaps London was not such a terrible place after all.

CHAPTER VI

The next day Rebecca paid a visit to her friend Harriet and was gratified to hear that Harriet was well enough to receive visitors. But when Harriet entered the drawing room of her home, Rebecca could only with difficulty conceal her shock. Miss Franks's face was much too pale, while the dark shadows under her eyes were two silent witnesses to a sleepless night.

"Dearest Harriet, are you certain you are well enough to see me?" Rebecca asked. "Or perhaps we should retire to your room."

"The change will do me good, I am sure. Only let us sit by the fire. I am so cold."

Rebecca joined her friend by the fireplace, even though in her estimation the day was much too warm for the strong blaze that was glowing red hot in the hearth. After she inquired about the health of Mr and Mrs Franks, who were thankfully both fully recovered, Rebecca informed her friend about the progress of Isaac, for every day brought some new and astonishing accomplishment. She then came to the object of her visit, advice for how to rectify her error concerning Miss Taylor.

"I wish my mind was not in such a muddle," said Harriet. "I am sure there must be some way to honourably employ Miss Taylor, but I cannot think what. Have you begun your sewing lessons with her?"

"We have arranged to meet later this afternoon."

"Perhaps an idea will occur to you while you are conversing."

Their conversation, which was so less animated than usual, was interrupted by a parlour maid, who brought in the tea things and then disappeared from the room.

"I shall not have anything," said Harriet, "but do have some refreshments, Rebecca. You will not mind if I treat you as a sister and let you pour out the tea yourself?"

"I should not mind at all, but I also have no appetite."

"Then perhaps I shall return to my room. I feel so dismally weak."

Before Harriet could ring for a servant to assist her, Rebecca insisted on providing that assistance herself. Mrs Franks, who met them on the stairway, also lent a supporting arm. When Rebecca was sure that Harriet was comfortably situated in her bed — a sentiment that was only secured after plumping up the pillows several times and rearranging the folds of the bed curtains so that the patient could have an unimpeded view of the window — Rebecca returned to her home. There, in contrast to the sombre, hushed tones of a home visited by illness, all was noisy, busy disarray.

"At last you are here," said Mrs Lyons, who was carrying in her arms a pile of old sheets. "Go to your room at once and search your armoire for any linen that is nearly beyond repair."

Rebecca gave her mother a puzzled look. It was not unusual for one of the many Jewish old clothes men to pay a visit to Devonshire Square, but it was usually the servants who collected the cast off clothing and linen of the family and handed the bundles over to the peddlers. She could not think why her mother would be involved in such a project, unless …

"Mama, is someone in the family sick? Is it Isaac? I will go to Bury Street at once!"

"You shall do no such thing," replied Mrs Lyon. "It is the children at the orphanage who are ill and need these things. Perl is waiting for you upstairs."

Rebecca flew up the stairs, determined to turn her wardrobe upside down in the effort to help the orphanage's children, for whom she had a special affection, since she had dreams of one day becoming a great benefactress and being in a position to shower the young wards with all kinds of delicious treats and other tokens of affection. Fortunately, though, Perl, who knew her young mistress very well, had already made a search of the shelves and drawers — in an orderly fashion — and selected the items which she thought might be called into service. The bundle only needed Rebecca's approval, which the young lady gave with all her heart, complaining only that the bundle was much too small.

When all the bundles of the family had been gathered together, the question arose as to who should convey them to the orphanage. Usually, that role would have fallen to Meshullen Mendel, but he had been engaged by Mr Lyon to perform certain tasks in the clock-making establishment on Cornhill Street and therefore was not available.

"I can assist Perl," said Rebecca. "Together we shall manage."

"I would prefer there was some male to accompany you," replied Mrs Lyon, glancing about her as though she half expected some heretofore unknown male child to step into the hall.

"I shall protect them," said six-year-old Joshua, sticking his thumbs into the pockets of his waistcoat.

"Are you certain Viscount Wellington can spare you?" said Rebecca, unable to resist the opportunity to rile her younger brother - who despite his tender years was an ardent follower of Wellington's exploits in the Peninsular Campaign—even though she knew in her heart that such behaviour was not suited to a young lady almost of the marriageable age.

Joshua replied by raising his foot in preparation for giving his elder sister a swift kick in the shin. However, Mrs Lyon leapt into the breach before this escalation of sibling hostilities could be accomplished. Standing staunchly in between the two warring sides, she thrust one large bundle into Rebecca's hands, a small one into the hands of Joshua, and then pointed to the door and said, "Go. Now!"

It was a pleasant walk to the orphanage, which was not far. When they reached it, the little group from Devonshire Square saw that other families were also contributing to the cause. For a moment, Perl, who was seldom cowed, held back.

"Perhaps the children's illness is more serious than we thought, Miss. I hope it's not the plague."

At the mention of the word "plague," Rebecca also lost her enthusiasm. But then she remembered the novels of Mrs Anne Radcliffe, whose heroines' sensibility might be delicate but whose mettle, when tested by a crisis, was made from steel, and she said, with what she hoped was suitably heroic pathos, "I shall take the things inside, Perl. You wait here with Joshua."

"Oh, no, Miss. I shall enter with you. But perhaps Joshua should remain outside. It would be a pity for the family to lose the two of you. The house would be too quiet to bear."

For once, Joshua made no complaint. The mention of plague had frightened him, as well. While Rebecca and Perl made their way to the entrance of the orphanage, he set up watch on a stone bench that sat near the railing. Fortunately, a small troop of toy soldiers had accompanied him, since his coat pockets made an excellent mess hall. He therefore took out a few of them and began to set them into position.

While he was engrossed in his war games, old Jeremiah Schneider, who had heard the news that he could come out of hiding, turned into the street, carrying his heavy bundle of ragged clothes and linens on his back. "Alt clo's!" the old man called out. "Buy or sell. Alt clo's! Alt clo's!"

As the old clothes man made his way down the street, a band of ruffians were coming up the street from the other end. "Alt clo's! Alt clo's!" they taunted, even going so far as to knock the hat off of the elderly man's head. While Jeremiah stooped over to pick up the hat from the gutter, one of the gang members gave the old man a push, which sent Jeremiah sprawling into the street.

They would have continued with their wicked sport had not General Well'ngone and a few of his boys appeared at that moment. Though the General and his boys were smaller than the rival gang, they knew how to produce a fierce noise. And so whooping and yelling at the top of their lungs, they charged the enemy—which quickly dispersed in a cowardly retreat.

While two of the General's boys helped Jeremiah to his feet, Well'ngone retrieved the old man's hat from the gutter. "Your brim has turned traitor, Mr Jeremiah. It has parted company with its crown," said General Well'ngone, as he regarded the battered hat with a woeful mien. "It is torn here in the front. Do you see?"

"Aye, tis seen better days," agreed the old clothes man. "I shall have to look for another."

"Just be sure you don't go looking for another one in the pocket of a Bow Street Runner."

"That wasn't my fault, General Well'ngone. You tell the Earl wasn't I that tipped off the law. I was feared for my own life, I was. They snatched my bundle—tore a good shirt, they did—and that's how they went and found the handkerchief. But I never said where I'd got the handkerchief from. You tell the Earl my words. It wasn't me that jabbered. My tongue was silent. My mouth was like a grave."

"Is that so? Then how is it that you are back on the street? If the law let you go, it must be because it is now measuring the noose to fit another man's neck."

"Begging your pardon, General, but in this instance I'm afeard you've heard it wrong. It was Mr Melamed that put in a good word for me, and a good coin to go with it, from what I heard."

"Well, make sure that tongue of yours stays silent, if you wish to continue to take tea with the Earl — if you follow my meaning."

"I understand you, General. My compliments to the Earl."

General Well'ngone and his companions went on their way. The old clothes man picked up his bundle, but when he tried to swing it upon his back he grimaced with pain.

Joshua, who had observed the entire scene from his seat on the bench, swept his soldiers into his pocket and crossed the street. "There is a bench over there, if you would like to sit down," he said to the elderly man.

"Thank you, sir. That is most of kind of you."

Joshua accompanied the old clothes man to the bench. Jeremiah, understanding that the child wished to say something, gestured to the other half of the bench and said, "There is room for two, sir, if you care to join me."

"Thank you, sir. I will."

"You are not one of the young orphans, I take it."

"No, sir. My name is Joshua Lyon. I live with my family in Devonshire Square."

"I am pleased to make your acquaintance, Mr Joshua Lyon. My name is Jeremiah Schneider and I live … well, let us just say that I live and not bother ourselves with the details."

"It must be hard work to be an old clothes man. Your bundle looks very heavy."

"Aye, tis heavy work, but it has its pleasures, too. Plenty of fresh air, and sunshine, there is - that is when it doesn't rain. Of course, it wouldn't suit for a young gentleman like you, but for someone like me, old clothes suit just fine."

Old Jeremiah laughed at his little joke, and Joshua joined him, but only to be polite. He did not see how such a life could be said to suit anyone, and so he said, "I do not wish to be impertinent, Mr Schneider, since we have only just now become acquainted. But may I speak freely?"

Jeremiah gazed down at his young companion and smiled. "I am at your service, sir."

"You see, I saw what happened to you. I was sitting here. And I heard those older boys taunt you. I should have said something, only, well, I am only six years old."

"I beg of you, sir, say no more. It was not your place to enter the brawl. And the good Lord did not forsake me, as you certainly saw, as well."

"Yes, I did see that, too. But my point is, sir, that perhaps if you did not speak so queerly, people would not taunt you. If you would say "old clothes" like an Englishman, perhaps you would be treated with more respect."

"Ald cloze?"

"No. Like this." Joshua then said the two words very slowly and very clearly: "Old clothes."

"Old clothes," the elderly man said, mimicking the child's careful enunciation.

"You can say it!"

"'Tis true, Mr Joshua Lyon. I can say 'old clothes' as fine as any Englishman when I am sitting on a comfortable bench and having a comfortable conversation with a gentleman like yourself. But in my profession, I must walk up and down the streets of London all day, and shout out my words one hundred times an hour, like this: Alt clo's. Alt clo's Alt clo's. You try it."

Joshua did try it, saying the two words as quickly as the old man. When his clear diction dissolved into something like the alt clo's of the old man's speech, he admitted defeat. "I see the problem," he said with true regret. Being unwilling, though, to give up his idea of helping the elderly man raise his position in the eyes of the world, he added, "Perhaps, then, you should consider changing your profession."

Jeremiah was about to explain that it was not an easy thing for an old man without capital to begin a new career. But then he recalled that Joshua was still a young child; the boy would have ample time to become acquainted with the ways of the world, a world were dreams were fleeting as youth itself, while disappointments endured for a lifetime.

* * *

While Joshua was engaged in conversation with Mr Schneider, Rebecca was speaking with Mr Maurice Muller, the orphanage's director. Mr Muller, who was of an excitable nature on even ordinary days, now fairly spun with anxious anxiety, turning from Rebecca to an assistant to a child and then back to Rebecca, like a top about to go out of control.

"Good heavens, no. There is no plague here, Miss Lyon. … Mr Greene, there is a draft in Room Five. See what the problem is and have it remedied. … As I was saying, Miss Lyon … Simon, can you not see that I am speaking with a lady? Do not interrupt."

Rebecca, recognizing the young messenger boy who worked in her father's clock-making establishment, assured Mr Muller that she could wait.

"Well, what is it, Simon? Speak up," said Mr Muller.

"It's Ezekiel, sir. He's taken bad again."

"What room?"

"My room, sir."

"I shall send someone to see to him. Now go back to bed. You must obey Mr Taylor's instructions."

Simon hurried off to his room, and Rebecca's eyes followed him. "Simon looks very pale, Mr Muller," she said. "If it is not the plague, what is wrong with the children?"

"I wish I knew, Miss Lyon. I wish I knew. At first Mr Taylor thought it was tainted food, although I assured him and Mr Melamed that we are most scrupulous about what we serve the children. Of course, if there were more money, we could be more generous with our helpings. But no child goes hungry in this orphanage and I do not take kindly to a stranger, even if he is a physician, suggesting that we would ever serve the children food that was dangerous to their digestive systems."

"Surely Mr Taylor did not suggest that you would do such a thing intentionally," said Rebecca, when she could finally insert a comment into the conversation.

"To be accused of carelessness is just as bad. Mrs Halberstein, our cook, who is a widow, you know — and it is against the Torah to oppress the widow, as I told Mr Melamed just a few minutes ago — broke down into tears when she heard what Mr Taylor said. 'Me, Mr Muller?' she cried. 'Me serve those poor orphaned children tainted food? The old physician, Mr Obadiah, would never have made such an accusation. May the Al-Mighty chop off my right hand, so that I can never chop another vegetable again, if I ever did such a thing, Mr Muller!' I cried with her, Miss Lyon. I can assure you, the tears were still in my eyes when I accosted Mr Melamed, who was standing in the very spot where, Miss, you are standing now. 'Mr Melamed,' I said, 'Mr Taylor must apologize at once.'"

"What did Mr Melamed say?" asked Rebecca.

"He said, 'Mr Muller, if it was not the food, what has made all the children ill?'"

"And do you know the cause, Mr Muller?"

"I? How should I know? I am not a physician."

"No, you are not," said an angry voice.

The little group turned to see who had spoken. Miss Elisheva Taylor stood before them, her eyes shooting sparks of defiance in the direction of Mr Muller.

"Miss Taylor! I did not … I thought … I …" Mr Muller nervously hopped from one foot to the other, a movement he resorted to whenever his agitation was extreme.

Miss Taylor ignored him and instead turned her attention to Miss Lyon and Perl, who were still hanging on to their bundles. "Are those clean sheets, Miss Lyon?" she asked. "May I take them? We are in desperate need of clean sheets and linen right now."

Rebecca was aware that she was included in the circle of Miss Taylor's anger, and she was sorry for it. Eager to make some sort of amends, she asked, as she and Perl handed over their bundles, "Are you helping with the children, Miss Taylor? That is so kind of you. And Mr Taylor must be very grateful for your assistance. I should like to help, too, if I would not be in the way."

A slight cough from Perl, who was aware of Miss Lyon's tendency to become ill herself when confronted with the sight of a sick person, alerted Miss Lyon to the need to qualify her statement, and so she said, "Of course, I do often turn green at the sight of unpleasant things. And sometimes I faint. But I could read to the children, or make them amusing drawings, if Mr Taylor thinks that would help their recovery."

The expression on Miss Taylor's face softened. "Thank you, Miss Lyon. I will ask Mr Taylor. And I am afraid we shall have to postpone our lessons until this crisis has passed. I am needed here."

"Of course, I understand."

As Miss Taylor turned to go, Mr Melamed appeared in the hall. "Ezekiel has been sick again, Miss Taylor. Can you attend to him?"

"I will go at once."

Mr Melamed next turned his attention to Mr Muller and, taking some bank notes from his pocketbook, said, "Make sure there are good fires burning in all the rooms day and night, until this illness has passed."

"Yes, Mr Melamed." The director of the orphanage took the bank notes and disappeared down a hallway, apparently eager to escape from the orphanage's benefactor as quickly as possible.

Mr Melamed bowed to Miss Lyon and was about to leave, when the young lady stopped him and said, "Mr Melamed, may I have a word with you?"

Mr Melamed, whose face was also showing the strain of the crisis that had overwhelmed the orphanage, bowed a second time. "How may I be of assistance, Miss Lyon?"

"I shall try to be brief, because I know you have so many affairs to attend to, but I have made such a tangle of things and I was wondering if there might be some way to make them right. You see, my family is aware that Mr Taylor and Miss Taylor are in need of financial assistance. My sister Hannah, Mrs Goldsmith, had devised a scheme that my father would pay Miss Taylor to give me sewing lessons. But then I told Miss Taylor that I would teach her how to draw if she would teach me how to sew and so then, of course, we could not offer to pay Miss Taylor for her sewing lessons because she would insist on paying me for my drawing lessons. Am I making myself clear?"

"Admirably clear, Miss Lyon. You would like to help Miss Taylor and her brother. Have you thought of another way to do so?"

"I have been wracking my brain for days, Mr Melamed, without success. But today I think I see a way out of the dilemma. If Miss Taylor will be assisting her brother here at the orphanage until the children are all well, could not the orphanage offer to pay her for her services?"

"The orphanage could, if the orphanage had the money to do so, Miss Lyon. But with so many additional expenses right now, I am afraid we must accept Miss Taylor's very kind offer to assist without expectation of remuneration."

"What if my father were to pay her wages?"

"Have you spoken to your father about this matter?"

"No, I have not had the time. But he did agree to pay for Miss Taylor to teach me to sew. Would it not be reasonable to assume that he would agree to this plan, instead?"

"I am on my way to the Great Synagogue now, for the afternoon prayers. Shall I speak to Mr Lyon for you?"

"If you would be so kind to do so, Mr Melamed, and to say that it was my idea. You see, my family was very upset when I interfered and upset their plans to help Miss Taylor."

Mr Melamed assured the young lady that she would receive full attribution for the excellent plan, and then hurried out of the orphanage, as he did not wish to be late for the prayer service.

If the Reader should wonder at Mr Melamed's high regard for one so young in years, I need only point out that this was not his first acquaintance with Miss Lyon and her attempts to assist when the community was in peril. True, her assistance did sometimes end in unlooked for and unfortunate complications. It was also true that the young lady did not successfully guess the identity of the spy ring that attempted to ensnare the unsuspecting Mr Franks — as explained in *The Ruby Spy Ring*, Mr Melamed had done that. But she had been correct in her suspicions that something out of the ordinary was going on in the Franks household, an investigative deduction that a less imaginative eye — one that had not been trained to see the world through the lens of a novel by Mrs Anne Radcliffe — would have missed. Therefore, even though Mr Melamed, who had not had the pleasure of being acquainted with Mrs Radcliffe's works, approached his investigative work from a very different perspective, he was not one to begrudge appreciation where appreciation was due.

* * *

When the afternoon services at the Great Synagogue had concluded, Mr Melamed drew Mr Lyon aside and soon received the clockmaker's assent to the plan concerning Miss Taylor. Yet if he had hopes of retiring to Baer's Coffee House for an hour of peaceful companionship in that kosher establishment—a thing Mr Melamed often did in the late afternoon, ever since his wife passed away and the silence of his stately rooms on Bury Street had become too burdensome—those hopes were quickly dashed.

First, he was accosted by Mr Jeremiah, who wished to thank his benefactor for rescuing him from the clutches of the men from Bow Street. "Try to stay out of trouble in the future," Mr Melamed replied.

"I will, sir. Thank ye, Mr Melamed."

During this short conversation a stranger, who had been standing in the courtyard of the Great Synagogue and anxiously examining the Jewish men who were leaving that venerable house of prayer, stepped forward.

"Mr Melamed, beg your pardon, sir," said the young man, whom Mr Melamed recognized as being in the employ of his business associate. "Mr Powell sends his compliments and asks if you could join him in Mayfair, at the home of Lady Marblehead." Then, upon seeing Mr Melamed's puzzled expression, the young man added, "It's urgent, sir. Mr Powell's carriage is waiting."

CHAPTER VII

Although the world that was centred upon the Great Synagogue and the world that was centred upon Mayfair were worlds apart in most ways, the physical distance between them was not so very far, especially when traveling in a comfortable carriage pulled by a team of strong horses. Mr Melamed therefore did not have much time to brood upon the cause of the summons he had just received. He assumed that his friend had not received bad news concerning his son; if that had been the case, the carriage would be traveling to Mr Powell's home. Mr Melamed therefore tried to recall all that he knew about Lady Marblehead.

This activity did not take long, since his affairs rarely took him to the drawing rooms of the non-Jewish gentry and neither he nor Mr Powell spent their time in gossip. And so when the carriage came to a halt, he was as much in the dark as when his journey had started.

The front door was opened to him at once and, to his surprise, a parlour maid led him not to the drawing room but further up the stairs, to Lady Marblehead's bedchamber. Mr Powell was in the room, as were a young man who looked like a gentleman and an elderly man whom Mr Melamed correctly assumed was a physician since he was fussing about the patient—Lady Marblehead, who was lying in the great four-poster bed and looking very pale.

Mr Powell had seen his business associate enter the sickroom and he immediately went over to Mr Melamed. "You must think it strange my asking you to be here," he said in a low whisper, "but the entire thing is exceedingly strange."

Mr Powell was about to lead Mr Melamed back out to the hallway, when Lady Marblehead opened her eyes and espied the new person who had entered the room. "Is that him, Powell? Is that your friend?"

"Yes, ma'am. But I beg of you not to exert yourself."

"Would you then have me remain silent? When a murderer is in the room?!"

Mr Melamed cast a hasty glance in Mr Powell's direction, but before Mr Powell could speak the elderly woman shrieked, "Yes, murderer! You Jews are all alike—you wish all Christians dead. Well, Jew, see what a Jewish doctor has done. He has murdered me! Murdered …"

A new wave of sickness prevented the elderly woman from continuing with her rant. While the physician attended to his patient and a very pale Mr Clyde hurried to the window, Mr Powell succeeded this time in leading Mr Melamed out of the room.

"My cousin is raving, of course, Melamed. No one suspects you. But do you know anything about a Jewish man who is supposedly newly arrived in London and claims to be a physician? Gabriel Taylor is his name. My cousin, Lady Marblehead, engaged his services a fortnight ago."

Mr Melamed stared. "I know the man personally. I have engaged him to be the physician at the Jewish orphanage."

"Well, for his sake, I hope all the children there are well."

"What do you mean?"

"It seems my aunt has been poisoned."

"What?"

"It is not my opinion. It is the opinion of the physician who is attending to her now. His name is Crawley. He was her physician for many years, and so I asked him to come when my aunt became ill. You understand that I hesitated to summon Mr Taylor, given the nature of my aunt's allegations."

"But surely you do not believe that a physician would poison his patients."

"I would hope not. But who is this Taylor? What do you know about him?"

"He studied medicine on the Continent, at Gottingen."

"He is a German fellow, then?"

"No. His family is English. But he grew up in Jamaica."

"Jamaica?" Now it was the turn of Mr Powell to stare.

At that moment, Mr Clyde, whose stomach could bear no more, rushed from the room and blindly sought out the privacy of his bedchamber.

Mr Powell's gaze went after the young man. "I wonder."

* * *

This time, Mr Melamed let nothing deter him from directing his steps to Baer's Coffee House. It was not physical nourishment that he needed, but sound advice—a commodity that could be found in abundance at that venerable kosher establishment thanks to the level head of the coffee house's proprietor, Mr Asher Baer.

Mr Melamed instructed the coachman of the hired carriage to come to a halt at the entrance to Sweeting's Alley, and he stepped down. While traversing the familiar narrow passageway on foot, he was unfamiliarly nearly knocked over by a person who was leaving the coffee house in a hurry.

"Beg your pardon, sir," said the person, who was about to make a hasty retreat when he recognized Mr Melamed and, in an instant, changed his mind. "But perhaps this unfortunate start to our acquaintanceship will end happily for all that. My name is Amos, sir. Perhaps you have heard of the enterprise I am proud to represent—Amos & Amos—remember the name, sir."

"Not now, Mr Amos," said Mr Melamed, who attempted to get past the tea merchant and through the coffee house's front door.

"If not now, then when, sir, may I ask? Our Sages asked it once, I ask it again. If not now, then when? When will your tea be as palatable to your pocketbook as it is to your stomach? If not now ..."

"See hear, Mr Amos," said Mr Asher Baer, who had heard the sound of voices on his doorstep and come outside, "do not bother my customers with your prattle. I will not allow it. And if you persist, I will return the two tins I bought from you."

"Neither my tea nor I will remain an instant where we are not wanted," replied Mr Amos, bowing to each of the men. "But mark my words, Mr Melamed, one day you will be coming to me. Amos & Amos. Remember the name."

Mr Amos went on his way, while Mr Baer escorted Mr Melamed to that gentleman's accustomed seat, which was located at the back of the coffee house. When a plate heaped high with roast beef and Mrs Baer's delicious potato kugel had been placed on the table, along with a cup of strong black coffee, Mr Baer accepted the invitation to join Mr Melamed at the table.

"How are the children at the orphanage?" asked Mr Baer. "Mrs Baer was ever so upset when she heard the news. She is upstairs making a large pot of beef bouillon now."

"I am sure it will be very much appreciated," replied Mr Melamed.

"Does the physician say what the cause is? It is not our business, strictly speaking, but having young children ourselves, if there is anything we can do to protect our children from contracting the ailment, Mrs Baer and I would naturally wish to do it."

"Mr Taylor thought some food might have been tainted, but now he is not so sure. Neither am I."

Mr Baer was silent. He knew that when Mr Melamed was ready, he would divulge what was on his mind. Meanwhile, Mrs Baer had come into the coffee room, to pay her respects to Mr Melamed. On her way to the back table, she espied the two tins of tea sitting where Mr Baer had left them, on one of the empty tables near the front door.

"Good afternoon, Mr Melamed," she said. "How are the children?"

"We were just discussing that, my dear," said Mr Baer. "But perhaps Mr Melamed would like to enjoy his dinner in peace."

"The kugel is delicious," said Mr Melamed. "I know you have sent the recipe to my cook, but for some reason it is never the same."

Although Mrs Baer was a woman with strong opinions, she was also a woman who knew when to hold her tongue. Therefore, although she might have commented that one could not expect a kugel prepared by a hired servant to reach the exalted level of a kugel lovingly prepared by the hands of a Jewish woman for her family and friends, she did not. If Mr Melamed was still unmarried, after the sudden and unexpected death of his beloved first wife, she felt partially to blame. She had spent many an hour thinking about the problem — for in her eyes there was no greater problem than a person deprived of the bliss of the marital state — and yet a suitable helpmeet for Mr Melamed had failed to materialize.

She therefore said, instead, "I shall be happy to send some kugel to Bury Street before Shabbos, Mr Melamed. I would send some to the orphanage along with the bouillon, if I thought the children's stomachs could tolerate it, the poor dears."

Mrs Baer then recalled the two tins of tea and said to her husband, "Where did that tea come from?"

"A new merchant, I could get rid of him in no other way. The tea was not expensive. Indeed, it was rather cheap. Perhaps we can have some with our supper tonight and see how it tastes."

"I am happy with the tea we already use, Mr Baer. But perhaps the orphanage would like it. Shall I send it with the bouillon, Mr Melamed?"

"That is very kind of you."

Mrs Baer returned to her kitchen, which was located on the floor above. Mr Melamed, who was sufficiently revived after his meal, felt ready to unburden his mind. First, though, he glanced around the coffee house to make sure that no one was sitting close enough to overhear the conversation. Fortunately, it was not an hour when the coffee house was filled with patrons, and so he could speak freely.

"Have you made the acquaintance yet of Mr Gabriel Taylor, the new physician?"

"I have not," replied Mr Baer. "Mrs Baer has met his sister."

"I wish you had. I would very much like to hear your opinion of him."

"You suspect something is wrong with his treatment of the children?"

"I did not, until today." Mr Melamed then described his summons to the home of Lady Marblehead and what had occurred in the sick room.

"The woman must be mad!" exclaimed Mr Baer, after he heard about the allegation of poison.

"I would dismiss what she said, as well, were it not for the discussion I had afterward with her previous physician, Mr Crawley."

"And what did he say?"

"He said that this was no common ailment of the stomach. The violence of the sickness, as well as its colour, which was a curious green, together with the patient's spasms — they all pointed to one thing, in his opinion. Lady Marblehead has been poisoned."

"Will she survive?"

"Mr Crawley believes so. At least, he is hopeful that he was called in time."

"But who would do such a thing? Surely no one can seriously believe that it was Mr Taylor. What on earth would he gain by poisoning his patient?"

"I do not know. But Mr Powell made a curious statement. He said that he hoped that the children at the orphanage were well."

Mr Baer glanced uneasily about the room before he spoke, "You think there might be a connection?"

"I am not a physician, but I was in the room when one of the children became ill. I saw the spasms. I also saw the colour of the liquid that was in the bowl, after the child had been sick. It was green."

"But why?" asked Mr Baer, truly shocked to hear this news. "Children … How could anyone do such a thing? He must be a monster!"

"We do not yet know that poison is truly the culprit, or that Mr Taylor is responsible. The cause may turn out to be something else entirely, and it could be a coincidence that the illness has struck several of Mr Taylor's patients."

"There is no such thing as coincidence, Mr Melamed, and you know it. It is the Al-Mighty Who orchestrates everything from Above, and if it is His wish to reveal Mr Taylor for what he is before he actually murders anyone, then we must do all that we can to bring him to justice."

"But first, we must satisfy ourselves that Mr Taylor is truly guilty of the crime."

"If we have time. Will not Mr Powell and Mr Crawley go to Bow Street and demand that Mr Taylor be arrested?"

"Mr Powell is prepared to give me time. I managed to convince Mr Crawley to wait as well. I told him that it would not do for it to get about fashionable London that physicians are poisoning their patients, and he accepted the argument. But we do not have much time. So far, no one has died. If that should change, G-d forbid …"

For a few moments the two men contemplated that gloomy thought. Then Mr Baer asked, "What do you propose to do?"

"First, I would like to obtain your opinion of Mr Taylor. Could you contrive to contract some illness, so that you have a reason to ask his professional advice?"

"I shall do it, but I shall not let him near my children."

"I understand. It would also be helpful if you could keep an ear open, here in the coffee house. Try to find out if others have become ill with a similar ailment. I have asked Mr Powell to do the same, in the drawing rooms that he is accustomed to visit. If we can prove that the ailment has affected others, who have no connection to Mr Taylor, then we shall have proved his innocence."

"And you feel certain that he is innocent?"

Mr Melamed silently considered the question before replying. "Only Hashem can know for certain," he said, finally. "I can only hope that no Jewish physician would knowingly cause his innocent patients harm."

CHAPTER VIII

It was no easy thing for Mr Baer, who had been blessed with excellent health, to put on a show of being ill. Nature apparently had compassion for him, though, because it came to his aid. During the night his youngest child, who was about to become the proud owner of his first tooth, awoke in considerable pain and refused to be comforted for several hours. Mrs Baer wisely argued that it would be best if Mr Baer stayed up with the child, so that he would look suitably haggard in the morning. He agreed, and she cheerfully went back to bed.

When morning came, and brought with it a hastily summoned Mr Taylor, the proprietor of the coffee house could truthfully complain that he was feeling uncharacteristically exhausted. "I have barely the energy to raise myself from this chair," he added woefully.

Mr Taylor performed his examination, and then said, "Thank G-d, there is nothing seriously wrong with you, Mr Baer. You are perhaps working too hard — a man of your age should not expect to do the work of a man of twenty, you know. I would therefore recommend that you try to work less and get more sleep. Perhaps you could hire someone to assist you in the coffee house. More fresh air would also do you good, so try to take some exercise out of doors. Other than that, I have nothing to recommend.

But should your condition worsen, let me know. Now, if you will excuse me, I must go to the orphanage. I assume you have heard that many of the children have taken ill."

"Yes, Mr Taylor, we have heard and we are praying for their speedy return to good health. Thank you for your advice. I shall try to follow it."

Later, when Mr Baer was sitting in the coffee house with Mr Melamed and Mr Powell, he recounted the details of his visit with the physician.

"More sleep, fresh air, exercise," Mr Melamed mused. "There is nothing harmful in that advice."

"No," Mr Powell reluctantly agreed. "Have either of you discovered more cases of this illness? I, for one, have not. Last night I called in at one dinner party, three card parties and two private balls, and fashionable London seems to be in the best of spirits and health."

"I have heard no talk in the City," said Mr Melamed.

"All that I was able to discover is that the Franks family was taken ill a few days ago," said Mr Baer. "Mr and Mrs Franks have fully recovered, but it seems that their daughter is still very weak. Mr Franks asked to speak to Mrs Baer about it. He did not come out and say that he was uneasy about the healing skills of Mr Taylor, but he thought it would do no harm to ask Mrs Baer's advice."

"What did she say?"

"She thought the diet recommended by Mr Taylor was sound. But she had a bit of the bouillon left, and so she gave some of it to Mr Franks to take home."

"Another patient who is not recovering," said Mr Powell.

"Yet Mr and Mrs Franks did return to health," Mr Melamed objected.

"Perhaps this poison affects only children, the elderly, and those who naturally tend to be weak."

"That is a possibility," Mr Melamed conceded.

"Have any children in the orphanage taken ill?" Mr Powell persisted.

Mr Melamed had not wanted to reveal this piece of information just yet, since he was sure that it could only further blacken Mr Taylor's reputation in the eyes of his friend. But he knew that Mr Powell would have other ways of finding out the information, and so he said that some of the children were ill.

"I should not like to have Mr Taylor as my physician," said Mr Powell as he rose to leave. "I suggest, Melamed, you find out if any of his other patients have become ill. I have a few inquiries I should like to make along a different line. I will let you know if anything comes of it. Good-day, Mr Baer."

When he had gone, Mr Baer stirred the remains of his coffee, seemingly absent-mindedly but in truth his mind was turning like the gears of a well-constructed clock.

"What are you thinking, Baer?"

"I am thinking about a story I once heard. It is about the Baal Shem Tov. You have a connection to the Chassidim, do you not?"

"I have through my daughter and her husband. They are followers of a Chassidic Rebbe who is currently living in Bohemia."

"I have no personal connection to them, but a person overhears a great deal in a coffee house. Most of it is not worth remembering, but this story stuck in my mind."

Mr Baer then proceeded to tell his tale: Once a famous physician learned that a patient, who was dissatisfied with the physician's treatment, had gone instead to seek help from the Baal Shem Tov, the founder of the mystical path called Chassidism. The angry physician stormed off to the Baal Shem Tov's home and said, "Since you seem to think you can heal better than I, let us agree to both undergo this test. I will examine you, and you will examine me. Whoever succeeds in best diagnosing his patient will be publicly proclaimed the better physician."

The Baal Shem Tov agreed to the challenge, and the famous physician went first. He tapped and prodded and studied the Chassidic Rebbe, but could not find a single trace of illness. "You are wrong, sir," said the Baal Shem Tov, "because in truth I am a very sick man. But my ailment is not a physical one. My sickness is that I have a constant yearning for Hashem."

It was then the turn of the Baal Shem Tov to examine the famous physician. He took the hands of the physician in his own, and gazed into the man's eyes for a very long time. "I see that once you lost something very valuable," said the Baal Shem Tov, "and that the loss made you very sad."

The physician was silent for several minutes, while he thought about what it was that he might have lost. He was about to say that the Baal Shem Tov was mistaken, when he recalled an incident that had occurred many years earlier. "You are correct," replied the physician. "I once had in my possession a very valuable diamond. It was stolen from me."

~ 79 ~

"That is your sickness," said the Baal Shem Tov.

The physician began to laugh. "You think I am still sick over a lost diamond? That is ridiculous!"

"You misunderstand me," replied the Baal Shem Tov. "My sickness is that I yearn for G-d. Your sickness is that you have forgotten that once you knew how to yearn."

When Mr Baer had concluded with the telling of his tale, he stirred his coffee some more. The gears of his mind were turning slowly while he attempted to connect the tale about the Baal Shem Tov with the goings-on in Mayfair and the Jewish orphanage.

"It is not an exact parallel, of course," said Mr Baer. "But I am caught by this word yearning. It makes me think that you can know something about a person's innermost thoughts, if you know what it is that he yearns for. Mr Taylor, for example, what does he want from life? Do we know?"

"A wife, a family, success in his profession, I would assume."

"We would assume, but do we know, Mr Melamed? On the outside, he appears to be like most young men. But what if his career means everything to him? What if he were willing to do anything to advance in that career, including conduct medical experiments with various poisons on innocent people?"

"I cannot believe that he would be so foolish as to try to poison an entire orphanage."

"Perhaps where he comes from no one cares about orphaned children. And, being a stranger to our community, perhaps he assumed that no one would care here, either."

Mr Baer took a sip from his coffee and grimaced. It had grown cold, and the remains were bitter. "Then there is Mr Powell," he said, pushing away the cup.

"Mr Powell?"

"It is only a theoretical question, Mr Melamed. But Lady Marblehead is a relative of his, and an elderly one, at that. Surely we can ask what it is that Mr Powell yearns for. And if it is something that would be obtained by the old woman's death."

* * *

While Mr Powell was being discussed in Baer's Coffee House, that gentleman was turning over in his mind a disturbing scenario of his own. Although he had no reason to be suspicious of Mr Clyde, he felt he could not ignore the fact that Lady Marblehead had taken ill not long after the young man's arrival in London.

He knew nothing about the young man, except that Mr Clyde was Lady Marblehead's great-nephew — nothing about the young man's character and nothing about his fortune, or lack of fortune, in Jamaica. He also knew nothing about what Lady Marblehead had promised Mr Clyde, although it seemed that some promise had been made. Otherwise, why had the young man appeared on the scene just then?

If Mr Clyde had been born and raised in England, finding out something about the young man would have been a relatively simple matter. Everyone in the gentry knew at least something about most everyone else — or knew someone who did.

Or, if our story had been set in Italy, the setting of many of Mrs Radcliffe's novels, and Mr Powell had been an evil Italian uncle, he would have simply thrown the young man into a dungeon. If that did not make Mr Clyde talk, there was always the rack.

But since Mr Powell was an English gentleman, and dungeons were not at his disposal, he was forced to proceed according to legal means. He therefore directed his steps to Lady Marblehead's solicitor, Mr Stanley Waters, a gentleman that he knew slightly.

When Mr Powell presented his card, Mr Waters's clerk assured him that Mr Waters would be at his service in a few minutes. The promise was fulfilled when the door to Mr Waters's private office opened and two gentlemen appeared. One was Mr Waters. The other was Mr Clyde.

Mr Clyde was looking affable as he said good-bye to the solicitor. With a still amused eye, he turned to Mr Powell and said, "You here, too, Powell? I hope you shall have better luck than I."

With that, the young man departed, and Mr Powell took his place in the solicitor's office. If Mr Waters was surprised by this second visit by a relation of his client, Lady Marblehead, he did not show it. Instead, he quietly took his seat behind his desk and asked how he might be of service.

"I shall not deny that my purpose is to discover the contents of my cousin's will," said Mr Powell. "Of course, I do not expect you to comply with my request. At least, not at first."

"May I assume then, sir, you have information that you hope will change my mind?"

"You are aware that there is a suspicion that Lady Marblehead was poisoned?"

Mr Waters removed his spectacles and wiped them with his handkerchief. "Yes, Mr Powell, I was just made aware of that fact. I was relieved to hear that Lady Marblehead survived this supposed assault upon her life."

"This time."

"You have reason to believe there will be a second attempt?"

"I have my suspicions. Whether those suspicions are valid are not I cannot presently say. It would help if I were familiar with the terms of Lady Marblehead's will."

Having replaced his spectacles on his head, Mr Waters began to softly drum his fingertips upon the top of his fine mahogany table. He had done well in his profession, and his rooms were furnished with furniture and pictures and rugs that would have been at home in the most exclusive London residences.

"Surely, Mr Powell, if you suspect foul play, you should report your suspicions to a magistrate. Why have you come to me?"

"I should not like to cast suspicion upon a young man, unless I was certain there was a good reason to suspect him."

"If you wish to know whether or not Mr Clyde will inherit under Lady Marblehead's will, I cannot answer you. That information is privileged, Mr Powell, as I am sure you know." He then added, "Why do you not ask Lady Marblehead?"

"I do not wish to unnecessarily worry her, not when she is still so ill. But if you cannot answer my first question, perhaps you can tell me if that is the reason why Mr Clyde paid you a visit—to ask if he will inherit?"

"This is most irregular, sir."

"Very well, I am sorry to have taken your time. I shall take your advice, and seek out a magistrate."

After Mr Powell left the office, Mr Waters called out to his clerk and said that he did not wish to be disturbed for the next half an hour. After he closed the door and turned the key, he took down from a shelf a box containing many papers. Some of the pages were quite old, dating back to the previous century. Others were of a more recent date, and it was to them that Mr Waters turned a careful eye.

When he had done with looking at them, he carefully placed all the papers back in the box, and the box back upon its place on the shelf. He then unlocked his door and called out to his clerk, "Find me a messenger boy."

When the boy was standing in his office, Mr Waters stared at the youngster with his sternest eye and said, "Are you familiar with a person who calls himself the Earl of Gravel Lane."

"Yes, sir."

"You know how to find him?"

"Yes, sir."

"And you know how to keep your mouth shut?"

"Yes, sir."

"We shall see if you speak the truth. Here is half a crown. If you deliver this message to the Earl and if you do not tell a soul about this conversation, when you come back this time next week I shall have another half a crown waiting for you."

"Yes, sir," said the boy, who ran out of the office, with the message clutched tightly in his hand.

Mr Waters went to the window and watched the boy's progress down the street. A boy like that was invisible in the crowded streets of London. No, that was not the problem. The difficult part was keeping his meeting with the Earl of Gravel Lane a secret. But should the boy talk, there were ways to handle that, as well.

CHAPTER IX

It was evening when Mr Taylor and his sister returned to their rooms on Bury Street. Miss Rebecca Lyon, who had been visiting the Goldsmith residence, was standing at the window of her married sister's drawing room when she spotted the brother and sister approach the building.

"They are here!" she called out to her sister Hannah, who was busy wrapping in paper a freshly baked cake.

"Not so loudly, Rebecca. They might hear you."

"Is the money from Papa inside?" asked Rebecca, as she peered inside the basket, which was filled with all sorts of delicious food.

"Yes, but remember, you are not to mention where the money has come from, or the food. The basket is from a grateful community. You must say no more."

They heard a door close above them. "We should give them a few minutes to take off their coats and hats," said Hannah. "You are certain you know what to say?"

Rebecca nodded her head.

"And do not remain in the room. When Miss Taylor takes the basket from you, leave at once. They must be exhausted from their work. This is not the time to babble on, as you sometimes do."

"That was when I was a child," Miss Lyon replied, a little stung by her elder sister's words. "But what if they will not accept the gift?"

"Then you must leave it on the table and depart at once." Hannah looked up at the ceiling and listened. "I think you can go upstairs now, Rebecca."

While Rebecca took the basket, Hannah took a candle, to light the way up the dark stairs. When she heard Rebecca knock upon the Taylors' door, she hastily retreated into her own rooms.

On the other side of the Taylors' door, the brother and sister heard the knock and looked at one another. "I am so tired," said Elisheva Taylor. "Perhaps we can ignore it."

"It might be a message from a patient," said Mr Taylor, who was also tired from the strain of the day's work, but felt that his professional duties must come first.

He was as surprised to see Miss Lyon standing in the hallway as she was surprised to see him. While he had not expected a visitor at all, she had expected to see Miss Taylor at the door.

"Is Miss Taylor at home?" Rebecca asked.

Mr Taylor opened the door to let her come inside. Miss Taylor had already come halfway across the room to see who had inquired for her.

"This is from a grateful community," Rebecca said, following her instructions to the letter. She tried to thrust the basket into Miss Taylor's hands, but that lady tried just as hard to refuse it. For several moments the two ladies were engaged in a silent struggle, which was resolved only when the basket slipped out of both their hands and fell to the floor. A loud crash made Rebecca look down at the basket in horror. "I hope it was not the eggs. Or the jug of milk. Although if it was both, I suppose you could make an omelette."

Miss Taylor started to laugh, as much from exhaustion as from the ludicrousness of the situation. "An omelette sounds delightful. Will you dine with us, Miss Lyon?"

"Oh no, I could not. The food is for you. From a grateful community. For all that you have done for the children at the orphanage," said Rebecca as she backed away and towards the door. "And please do not tell anyone that I dropped the basket."

"We shall not tell a soul," said Mr Taylor, who was by then also laughing. "Your dreadful secret is safe with us."

Miss Lyon raced down the stairs, not caring that it was dark or that she might tread upon a mouse. When she reached her sister's door, she stood beside it for several minutes, until she had composed herself.

"You are back!" said Hannah, gazing with a happy eye at Rebecca's empty hands. "And they accepted the food! You have carried it off successfully, Rebecca. I am proud of you."

Rebecca decided not to contradict her sister by revealing the circumstances concerning the dropped basket. Instead, she allowed herself to bask in the glow of Hannah's compliments. Even Isaac beamed at her with a gurgling smile, as though he wished to say, "And I am proud to have you for an aunt!"

In the rooms upstairs, the Taylors were unpacking the basket. Their tiredness was forgotten in the excitement of opening the paper wrappings and discovering the various dishes that were sitting inside. Fortunately, only a small pot of jam had cracked during the fall to the ground, but it had not received a hard enough blow to completely destroy the container. However, when Miss Taylor discovered the paper wrapping that contained coins inside, her joy dimmed.

"Do you think I should accept this, Gabriel?" she asked, showing the coins to her brother.

"Ordinarily, I would say that you should not. But since you have been working such long hours, and the work has been so disagreeable, I do not see why you should not use the money to buy yourself a new hat or pair of gloves after this ordeal is over."

"If I keep it, I shall save the money for my dowry," replied Miss Taylor, placing the money in a drawer. "Who do you suppose has done this, Mr Melamed or the Lyon family?"

"Perhaps both."

"Whoever it was, I do not think they meant it as charity. I think the community really does appreciate you, Gabriel, no matter what Mr Muller or that cook at the orphanage says."

"I hope so. I only wish I knew what was making the children ill."

"Some of them are recovering."

"I am worried about Ezekiel. He is so small. I do not know if he will survive another bout, if he should become ill again."

"Let us not think of that tonight," said Miss Taylor. "You need to consider your health, as well. Which shall we have for our supper, the meat pie or the roasted chicken?"

* * *

A carriage drove up to a dark house located on Gravel Lane. Carriages were not an accustomed sight in that part of London, but it was a neighbourhood where people knew that it was in their best interest to mind their own business. Therefore, if anyone did draw aside their ragged curtain to peer through a dirt-caked window pane at the sound of the carriage wheels, to steal a glimpse of who might be sitting inside the vehicle, they quickly let that curtain fall when they saw the familiar silhouette of General Well'ngone step into the lane and stride up to the carriage door.

"I wish to see the Earl, not you," a voice inside the carriage hissed.

"The Earl does not leave his rooms, sir. Everyone knows that. Either come inside, or discuss your business with me."

The voice inside was heard to mutter a mild oath, but the carriage door was opened wide enough for General Well'ngone to slip inside.

"The Earl sends his compliments."

"I do not care two bits for the Earl's compliments, and you can tell him that," replied Mr Waters, for that was indeed him wrapped inside several layers of coats and scarves, despite the warmness of the night. "I did the Earl a favour once, which saved him from the gallows. You will kindly remind him of that fact, and tell him that the time has come for him to repay the debt he owes me."

The Earl was enjoying his evening repast of stale bread soaked in ale when General Well'ngone returned. Although it was not his habit to discuss business concerns while eating, the distressed look on the General's face made him inquire about the cause of it.

"The man's gone off his chimney," said the General. "It must be all those years sitting in a dark room, scratching away with those quill pens. It's not healthy, in my opinion, neither the scratching nor the sniffing of all that ink."

"Never mind the health of Mr Waters. What was the purpose of his visit?"

"He wants us to break into his rooms."

The Earl, who was about to put a morsel of food into his mouth, stopped and stared at his aide-de-camp. "I presume he has a reason for his request."

"He wants us to steal some papers. He says he will tell us exactly where they are, so we can sneak in and out in no time. He'll leave open a window."

"I hope you informed Mr Waters that sneaking in and out of rooms is not a service that we provide for our clients."

"I did, but he was insistent that you owe him a favour."

The Earl returned his attention to his fork, as though the bit of stale bread was a rare and wondrous delicacy. "And I insist that we do not break into people's homes or places of business. He must find someone else."

"He says that if you don't do it, a Jew will go to the gallows."

"Did he mention which Jew?" the Earl asked, taking out his quizzing glass to examine the fork more closely, to be sure that an insect had not joined him for supper. And if he was concerned that the Jew in question was him, he did not show it.

"It's the new sawbones, the one who is at the orphanage."

"What's he done, poisoned his patients?" The Earl laughed at his little joke, but he stopped when he saw that the General was looking serious. "Is that what Waters is saying? That a Jewish physician is killing off his patients? How very medieval of him. How exactly is our Jewish doctor supposed to be doing it? Poisoning wells?"

"Waters didn't mention anything about wells," replied the General, "but he did say that he has in his possession an interesting piece of information concerning Mr Taylor. If he goes to the gallows, he's taking the Jewish doctor with him."

* * *

Mr Melamed sat in his library. A book and a glass of wine sat on the table beside his armchair. A refreshing spring breeze was bringing a welcome draught of cool air into the room. It was a near perfect night. But he could not enjoy it, for his heart was not at ease.

His conversation with Mr Baer had disturbed him. It was impossible for him to entertain the notion that Mr Powell would murder an elderly relation for money. He knew his friend too well. Yet Mr Melamed also knew, in his heart, that people had murdered for less. Perhaps Mr Powell was in some sort of financial difficulty (a person did not always confide such things to even the closest friend), and he had been counting upon the money from the Marblehead inheritance to rescue him from an unpleasant situation. Or perhaps it was the son who had gotten into trouble. It would not be the first time that a father ransomed his own honour to save a son and heir from disgrace. Was that what Mr Powell yearned for, at this moment, a release from some financial difficulty? But even if that explained the attempt to poison Lady Marblehead, it did not explain the wave of sickness at the orphanage.

And what about Mr Taylor? What did that young man yearn for? At this hour, Mr Taylor was most likely in his rooms in the building next door, perhaps already fast asleep after a long and exhausting day. If he was dreaming, of what stuff were his dreams made of? Was he dreaming of a fame that could only come with some heretofore unimagined scientific discovery? Was he willing to risk every moral scruple to achieve that glory? That too seemed impossible. When Mr Melamed had interviewed Mr Taylor, before entrusting him with the position at the orphanage, he had been impressed by the young physician's idealism and maturity. But was that initial impression now clouding Mr Melamed's judgment? Was it because he had been the one to recommend the young man that he found it so difficult to consider the notion that perhaps he had erred?

It was a much more comfortable notion to place the blame at the door of the newcomer to London, Mr Clyde. It was certainly easy enough to assume that the young man needed money; most young men did. But what connection could Mr Clyde have with the orphanage? It was the same problem as with Mr Powell.

That brought Mr Melamed back to Mr Taylor, who was the only one of the three men to be connected with both the orphanage and Lady Marblehead. He would need to find out more about the young man, but how? Poison was not a subject that arose naturally in a conversation.

The night breeze beckoned to Mr Melamed. He rose from his chair and went to the window to greet it. The view from the back of his library looked out upon an alleyway that was usually dark and quiet at this hour. Yet on this night there was a light shining in one window. It came from a group of low buildings that huddled against the back wall of the narrow passageway. Mr Melamed recognized its location, because he owned the buildings and he had rented one of the rooms to Mr Taylor. The young physician had requested a place where he could conduct his scientific experiments without disturbing his sister.

Mr Melamed knew what he must do. He must engage someone to spy upon his tenant. The thought was distasteful. Just the thought of it made him yearn to close his eyes to the whole affair. No, that was not true; that was only the tiredness speaking. He had a responsibility to the children.

But if he did not yearn to escape from the problems of the community, what did he yearn for? If the Baal Shem Tov were to enter the library at the moment and examine him, what secrets would that holy man discover? That since his wife's death he had become, like the physician in Mr Baer's story, a person who had forgotten how to yearn?

* * *

Simon, who was lying on his bed at the orphanage, was not enjoying the night breeze, since the window in his room was firmly closed so as not to let in a draft. He was feeling much stronger—he had not been sick once the entire day—but, like Mr Melamed, his heart was troubled. He threw off his coverlet and tiptoed over to the bed where Ezekiel was sleeping, to make sure that the child was still breathing. He was worried about Ezekiel, who seemed to be getting weaker with each passing day.

Simon and Ezekiel may not have been brothers by blood, but the two boys had become like brothers by circumstances. They had shared a room in the orphanage for more than a year, during which time they shared their sorrows, their fears, and their hopes. Since Ezekiel was a good two years younger than Simon, the older boy felt responsible for his young friend. Most days, this was not such a difficult burden to bear; it meant making sure that Ezekiel said his prayers and washed his hands and learned his letters. But ever since this illness had struck the orphanage, Simon had felt uneasy. He would pull through, he knew. He was less certain about Ezekiel. A whole evening had passed without Ezekiel taking an interest in the stories that Simon made up for his entertainment. And a whole day had passed with Ezekiel taking no more than a swallow-full of food. Even the sawbones and the sawbones's sister were looking worried.

Such were his thoughts when he heard a tap on the window. He recognized the bicorne hat outlined against the glass, and ran over to push the window open.

"General Well'ngone, you mustn't come inside," he whispered. "There's sickness here something awful."

"That's why I've come, Simon. What's making the boys so green?"

"I don't know."

"Doesn't the new sawbones say?"

"No. He just looks worried." Simon glanced over to Ezekiel's bed, looking worried himself.

General Well'ngone followed Simon's glance with his own sharp eyes. "Do you think the sawbones is helping Ezekiel? What's your opinion, Simon? You're a smart one."

"I like him. I like Miss Taylor, too. That's his sister. I heard her crying out in the hallway, after she told me and Ezekiel good-night. That's a sign a person wants to help, don't you think, General, when a person cries for you?"

Before the General could reply, Ezekiel began to stir in his bed. "Mama," the boy whimpered softly. "Mama."

Simon went over to the bed and took the child's hand. "Hush, Ezekiel. Go back to sleep."

"I heard voices, Simon. Who's here?"

"It's me, Ezekiel, General Well'ngone. The Earl sends his compliments and his wishes for your recovery to good health."

Ezekiel tried to reply, but he was too weak.

"Please give the Earl our thanks, and tell him that Ezekiel has every intention of recovering," said Simon, with more heartiness than he felt.

"Of course, he will," said General Well'ngone. "I can use a sharp lad like Ezekiel, when he gets a bit older."

"No, General, I've got other plans for the boy. Did you know that Ezekiel can already read aloud the letter A?"

"No, you don't say?"

"I do say. He can spot an A even if there are a hundred other letters on the page. I reckon that with his brains, someday Ezekiel may be a solicitor's clerk, or even a solicitor himself. You'd like that wouldn't you, Ezekiel? But you'll have to wear one of them big powdered wigs when you're strutting around in court and jabbering with the judge."

Ezekiel smiled, and then he closed his eyes and drifted back off to sleep.

* * *

"Well?" said the Earl of Gravel Lane, when the General returned from his visit to the orphanage.

"Simon seems to think that the sawbones is worth saving."

If there had been a fire burning in the Earl's drawing room, which was damp even on the hottest days, due to the water that seeped in through the walls and the floorboards, he would have gazed into its cheerful flames. But since his hearth was cold and dark, it was into that emptiness that he looked, while he communed with his thoughts.

CHAPTER X

The first call that Mr Melamed paid the next morning was to the residence of Mr Powell. As that gentleman was still breakfasting, but would be done with his meal shortly, Mr Melamed was shown into the library. Usually, Mr Melamed would have taken a book from a shelf and sat down in his usual seat. This morning, however, he noticed there were papers sitting on Mr Powell's desk, and even though he despised himself for doing it, he walked softly across the plush Turkey carpet to the desk.

He saw at once a page filled with jottings—the names of various properties, followed by various sums. Columns of figures had been added up, scratched out, and rearranged, only to be scratched out again. The reason for this exercise, Mr Melamed presumed, was the letter from Mr Powell's son, which Mr Melamed saw and quickly read, before his conscious could prevent him from doing the deed.

He was sorry for his friend, and sorry for the young man. Vast fortunes, as well as ancestral estates, were lost every year by young men who learned the value of money too late. But if Mr Powell were trying to pay off his son's gambling debts in an honourable manner—as those columns of figures seemed to suggest—surely he would not stoop to trying to murder his wealthy relation.

Mr Melamed heard footsteps in the hallway and quickly returned the letter to its place. By the time Mr Powell entered the room, he was seated in his chair.

"You are here early," said Mr Powell. "I hope there is not more bad news."

"No, I have come to ask for your help. I should like to speak with Lady Marblehead's servants, to find out more about the day when she became ill."

"I can do nothing without Lady Marblehead's permission, but I can go with you and see if I can persuade her. Shall we walk? The house is not far, hardly worth the bother of preparing the carriage."

"Before we go, I thought it would be helpful if I could go over the events of the day with you, Powell, if you do not mind."

Apparently, Mr Powell did mind, since the muscles in his face tightened. The moment passed quickly, though, and he sat down in a chair opposite Mr Melamed.

"I suppose you cannot help but include me in the circle of suspects," said Mr Powell. "I would do so, if I were to hear this story in my club. You may as well know that my son, Thomas, has managed to dispose of a large part of his fortune before he has even inherited it. Gambling debts—you are lucky you never had sons, Melamed. If Boney does not succeed in ruining England's economy, these infernal card games will."

Mr Melamed, who despite his great affection for his two daughters had often prayed for a son to join his family circle, did not feel he was lucky at all, and he was certain that Mr Powell did not truly feel that way, either. However, he was relieved that his friend had revealed the contents of Thomas Powell's letter himself. He therefore said, "If there is anything I can do to help, you know that I will."

"Thank you, but I prefer to poison my cousin instead." Mr Powell gave a bitter laugh at his attempt to make a joke. Then he said, "I do not know how much I recall about that afternoon. I believe I was here, in my library, when I received the message to come to my cousin's house at once. When I arrived, the servants were quite naturally distressed. My cousin had been violently ill and they did not know how to stop the convulsions."

"They had not sent for a physician?"

"No. Apparently my cousin already suspected that Taylor had poisoned her, and so they were hesitant to send for him."

"Did Lady Marblehead ever say why she suspected it was Mr Taylor?"

Mr Powell looked uncomfortable. "It seems that at first my cousin was very pleased with Mr Taylor. When she learned that he grew up in Jamaica, she showed him a pearl bracelet that came from somewhere in the Caribbean. According to the family lore, it had belonged to Captain Henry Morgan, the pirate. Whether he lost it at the gaming table or he used it to pay for liquor during one of his drunken sprees, no one knows. But the pearls are quite good, and even without the pirate story they would fetch an excellent price, should the family ever want to sell them."

Mr Melamed noted that his friend had said "the family," and not "Lady Marblehead." But he did not mention this, saying, instead, "And so when she became ill, Lady Marblehead suspected that Mr Taylor had poisoned her to obtain the bracelet?"

"Yes. I suppose it sounds ridiculous to us, but I imagine that Lady Marblehead was frightened. She truly was violently ill, you know."

"If she suspected that someone wished to rob her, why did she not suspect her lady's maid of taking the jewels?"

"Jeanette—that is the woman's name—had left my cousin's service the week before, or so Smithern informed me. Lady Marblehead has not yet found a replacement and so the parlour maid has been performing Jeanette's duties, as well, temporarily."

"Let us continue. When you arrived, what did you do?"

"I went upstairs, to my cousin's bedchamber. When I saw how serious her condition was, I sent at once for Mr Crawley. I had heard his name mentioned by my cousin. He had been her physician for many years."

"Did Lady Marblehead ever mention why she had engaged a new physician?"

"Not that I recall."

"She never mentioned that she was unhappy with Mr Crawley, perhaps because of something he had said or some treatment he had performed?"

"I think I see where you are headed, Melamed, but I do not think that Mr Crawley was angry at Mr Taylor for taking away his patient. My cousin was surely not an easy patient to attend to. There was nothing seriously wrong with her health, from what I can infer, but she desired company and attention and I can imagine that she detained Mr Crawley for much longer than was necessary. It must have been frustrating for him, especially on days when he had many other patients to visit."

"Did you stay in Lady Marblehead's bedchamber until Mr Crawley arrived?"

"I was there for most of the time. Of course, I had to go down to the drawing room to compose the message to Mr Crawley. Lady Marblehead did not keep pen and ink in her bedchamber."

"And so she was alone during that time?"

"No. Mr Clyde had excused himself from the room when I arrived. He returned as I was going downstairs. At least, he said he was going back to the sick room. I do not know if he did so immediately."

"So you wrote the message to Mr Crawley. Then what happened?"

"If my memory is correct, I went down to the kitchen to speak with the cook. My first thought was that perhaps Lady Marblehead had eaten some tainted food. I therefore thought it might help the physician, when he arrived, if I knew what she had recently eaten. Of course, it took some time to get the information from the cook, as she was very upset. I believe I was going back up the stairs when Mr Crawley arrived."

"And was the room the same when you came back to it?"

"What do you mean?"

"Had anything been taken from it, or rearranged—perhaps a glass, or the remains of a meal?"

"You are asking if Mr Clyde removed anything from the room, such as a piece of poisoned sponge cake?"

"I see your point, Powell. If something she ate had contained poison, the dish or the cup would have been in the dining room or the drawing room. But the poison might have been placed in a sleeping draught, if Lady Marblehead was accustomed to taking one before she retired for the night."

"I have no information about that. And I have no idea if Mr Clyde did anything to the room, while I was gone. My full attention was engaged by my cousin and the physician."

"Yes, I can understand that." Mr Melamed was silent for a few moments. He then asked, "Do you know if Lady Marblehead also showed this pearl bracelet to Mr Clyde?"

"I do not know."

"Do you know if the bracelet is still in Lady Marblehead's jewellery box?"

Mr Powell's eyebrows shot up. "Perhaps we should find out."

* * *

Lady Marblehead was not at all pleased by the idea of her servants being questioned, or so she said. Mr Melamed thought he signs to the contrary; the eagerness in her eye—perhaps in anticipation that such an event would prove to be entertaining—belied the vehemence of her verbal objections. In the end, though, she relented.

Mr Melamed had made the decision not to mention at first his suspicion that the pearl bracelet had gone missing. If he had broached the subject to Lady Marblehead, he was certain there would be a hue and cry. Once that happened, he was equally certain the servants would feel under suspicion for taking the bracelet and refuse to talk. It was better to first sort out their impressions of the fateful day when

Lady Marblehead had taken ill; he could question the servants again, about the bracelet, should the need arise.

In truth, the servants did not have much to add to Mr Powell's account, but Mr Melamed wrote down what each one said, while Mr Powell listened. The parlour maid had been the one to discover that Lady Marblehead had taken ill. "The mistress was slumped down in her chair, holding her stomach, and moaning piteously," the girl said.

"Which chair?" asked Mr Melamed.

"That one, sir." The girl pointed to the chair in the drawing room where Lady Marblehead often sat.

"Was this before she dined, or after?"

"The tea things were still on the table, sir."

"Was she having tea alone?"

"I believe Mr Clyde had had a cup with Lady Marblehead."

"But he was no longer in the room when you discovered that Lady Marblehead was ill?"

"No, sir. He sometimes went out in the afternoon. I believe he was upstairs changing his coat."

"Why do you believe he joined Lady Marblehead for tea?"

"Well, sir, there were two cups on the tray and they looked as though they had both been used. Although sometimes Lady Marblehead will finish the leftover tea in the cups herself, after the guests have gone. It's another one of her economies, she says."

Mr Powell tried very hard not to laugh, as he envisioned his cousin greedily gulping down the remains of the tea, before the tray was taken away. He dearly hoped that when he reached his cousin's age that he would still have full control over his faculties, and not descend to playing childish games, as the elderly sometimes did.

Mr Melamed let the last comment go by without saying anything that might be construed as a lack of respect for Lady Marblehead. Instead, he asked, "What happened after you discovered that Lady Marblehead was ill?"

"I asked milady if she would like to be taken upstairs to her room, and when she said yes I called to Mr Smithern, the butler, to help me."

"Did you remain with Lady Marblehead or go back downstairs?"

"I wanted to stay with milady, but Mr Clyde came in and he said he would stay with the mistress."

"Did Mr Clyde mention anything about feeling ill?"

"No, sir."

"What did you do after you left the sick room?"

"I went downstairs and cleared away the tea things."

"I suppose the cups and other things were washed before the physician arrived?"

"Oh, yes, sir. Cook does like to keep her kitchen tidy."

The cook, when she was summoned, was determined to say as little as possible, but her natural loquaciousness soon overcame her initial reticence. She had remained in the kitchen, not because she lacked feelings for a sick person but because she was not good in the sick room. "We must know where our talents lay, sir. Mine are in the kitchen, and it would be no good to anyone for me to pretend otherwise."

"Do you recall what was served for tea that afternoon?" asked Mr Melamed.

"Lady Marblehead was fond of a piece of sponge cake, sir, but I always put some bread and butter on the tray, as well. There might have been some seed cake left from the day before, but I cannot be sure."

"Did you notice if Lady Marblehead ate alone, or if Mr Clyde joined her?"

"I might have noticed it then, sir, but I'm sure I don't recall now."

"Was it the custom of the household for the servants to eat what was left on the tray, for your tea?"

"No, sir. Mr Smithern is not fond of sweet things and so I'll sometimes cook up an egg or cut us a slice of bread and cheese. We have it with a drop of ale, since none of us are fond of the new tea blend that milady had us purchase."

"Do you know why your mistress had you purchase the new blend?"

"It is cheaper, sir. I do not object to economizing, sir, but in my opinion there is such a thing as taking a thing too far, especially when a beverage tastes more like dishwater than a proper cup of tea. And milady does not object to our drinking ale instead of tea, so long as it is just a drop."

This time it was Mr Melamed's turn to try not to smile. He suspected that the cook was quite happy with the arrangement, which might include a "drop" of port from time to time, as well.

"So none of you ate from any of the dishes that were on the tray?" he asked.

"No, sir."

Mr Smithern contributed the information that Lady Marblehead had received no visitors that day, except for Mr Taylor, who had paid a call in the morning.

"At what time?" asked Mr Melamed.

"I believe it was 10:30 when he arrived. The clock in the hall was chiming the half hour."

"Did Mr Taylor usually pay a call at that time?"

"The time varied, sir, according to Lady Marblehead's convenience."

"Was Lady Marblehead not feeling well? Is that why Mr Taylor was summoned?"

Mr Smithern who had been politely helpful until then, grew silent.

"Come, man," said Mr Powell, growing impatient. "Someone may have tried to poison your mistress. This is no time to stand on ceremony. I will take the responsibility for what you say, should it in any way be interpreted as showing disrespect to Lady Marblehead."

"Well, then, sir, I would not exactly say that Lady Marblehead was unwell. But the new physician had recommended some changes in her diet and I believe milady wished to discuss a few things with Mr Taylor that she had read in a pamphlet. Lady Marblehead has always been very interested in matters pertaining to health and the medical profession."

Mr Melamed could envision the scene: the young physician, eager to tend to his real duties, but forced to listen politely to the ramblings of the elderly woman. It was no wonder that Mr Crawley had not minded when his services were deemed no longer necessary.

"Who was it that thought to summon Mr Powell, after Lady Marblehead was taken to her bedchamber?"

"I took the liberty of doing that, sir. Of course, I informed Lady Marblehead of my intention."

"And she did not object?"

"She was very ill, sir. I only stated my intention and left to find a messenger."

"Who else was in the room?"

"Mr Clyde, sir."

"I understand that Lady Marblehead's lady's maid has left her service."

"That is correct, sir."

"Did she give a reason?"

"She wished to marry, sir."

"She is a young woman?"

"Not so very young, but I believe she had been saving her earnings for several years so that she and her intended could buy an inn somewhere. She had had enough of being in service, she said."

"Do you have her address?"

"No, sir. She said she would write, when she was settled in her new home."

After the butler left the room, Mr Melamed conferred with Mr Powell concerning the best way to approach Mr Clyde. It was a ticklish business, since Mr Clyde was both a relative of Lady Marblehead and a guest in the house.

"Perhaps we should first ascertain if the pearl bracelet is still in my cousin's jewellery box," suggested Mr Powell.

They went off to find Lady Marblehead, who was sitting in the morning room, where she was still stewing over the ignominious treatment she had received at the hands of Mr Powell and Mr Melamed; for after she had allowed herself to be persuaded to permit the questioning of her servants, she had been dismissed from her own drawing room while Mr Melamed interviewed them. When the two gentlemen entered the morning room, she therefore glared at them and said, "Well, Powell, may my servants go on with their work, or must the house be topsy-turvy all day?"

"We thank you for your forbearance, ma'am," said Mr Powell, "and must trouble you for a little while more. Would you feel well enough to accompany us to your bedchamber?"

"My bedchamber is not a public exhibition room!" she retorted.

"Then perhaps you would allow me to bring down your jewellery box, so that we may examine its contents here."

"Are you suggesting that I have been robbed, as well?"

"At the moment, it is only a theory, Lady Marblehead," said Mr Melamed.

As she rang the bell, Lady Marblehead turned her head to conceal the smile that threatened to give away her renewed interest in the morning's activities. When the parlour maid came into the room, she instructed the girl to fetch the box.

"We will also need the key, ma'am," said Mr Powell. "I presume you keep the box locked."

"You presume rightly, Powell," said Lady Marblehead with a smirk. "But I am not so foolish as to leave the key laying in a drawer by the box. I always keep it with … me …" Lady Marblehead had unpinned a pocket that was attached to her dress and was rummaging through its contents, first calmly and then with more frantic motions. "It is gone!" she said at last, as she looked from one man to the other.

When the jewellery box had been brought into the room, it was soon discovered that the box was closed but unlocked. With a trembling hand, Lady Marblehead began to look through the drawers and compartments.

"What am I looking for, Powell?" she asked. "The diamonds are here, so is the emerald ring."

Before Mr Powell could answer, Mr Melamed said, "We would prefer, Lady Marblehead, if you would tell us if you have noticed if anything is missing."

Lady Marblehead did not object, only now she was not enjoying the situation. As she opened each compartment, her hands trembled anew. When she closed each one, she sighed with relief. The examination was almost completed when she pulled out a round jeweller's box and removed the lid.

"It is gone!" she screamed, almost falling from her chair. "I have been robbed! Robbed!"

The last word faded into a sob, and Mr Melamed had pity for the woman. Whatever her foolishness, she had truly suffered during the last several days.

When she had quieted down, Mr Melamed asked, "What was in the box, milady?"

"A pearl bracelet. A priceless pearl bracelet. It has been in my family for generations. I cannot believe it is gone." But as she stared into the box, and realized that its empty state was not an illusion, her strength returned. "Who has taken it, Mr Melamed?" she demanded. "Do you know?"

"Anyone in your household might have taken the key, milady. You were very ill. People were going in and out of the sick room at all hours."

"You cannot fool me, sir. You came to my house knowing the bracelet was missing. Who do you think took it?"

"That is obvious," said Mr Clyde, who had heard his great-aunt scream and entered the room unnoticed. "You suspect me. Is that not so, Mr Melamed? And do not be surprised that I know who you are. Smithern apprised me that you were here. Hello, Powell. Hello, auntie. I am sorry you have had another shock."

"Well? Did you take my bracelet?" asked Lady Marblehead.

"My dear aunt, think for one moment, please. Let us say that I did try to poison you. Would I have gone to all that trouble for just one bracelet? Not I! I should have taken the whole box and run off to the Continent, where I could sell just one jewel a year and still live in a grand style."

"You would do it, too," said Lady Marblehead, smiling now, "if you had half the courage that your grandfather had. But you are like my sister, pretty to look at but no gumption."

Mr Clyde turned to Mr Melamed and said, "Is there anything else you would like to ask me? I have promised to go riding in the park, and I do not wish to be late."

"Have you any idea who might have taken the bracelet?"

Mr Clyde thought for a moment. "Well, that depends. If we assume that the thief was looking for anything that he or she could grab. "

"I do not think so," said Lady Marblehead. "Why would the person pass over the diamonds, which are worth much more?"

"Very well," Mr Clyde continued, "let us suppose that the thief wished to steal that bracelet in particular. We must ask ourselves why."

"And when we ask ourselves that question, will we find an answer?" asked Mr Powell, his distaste for the young man growing with every passing minute.

"We might," said Mr Clyde. "For one thing, the bracelet would have had to be stolen by someone who knew of its existence—and knew in which compartment it was hidden. I happen to have known both these things, since when my aunt showed me the bracelet I saw her remove it from her jewellery box."

"Mr Taylor saw me remove it from my jewellery box, too!" exclaimed Lady Marblehead. "Why did I ever trust that scoundrel!"

"Have you any more questions to ask me, Mr Melamed? Or may I leave?"

"Of course, you may leave, Clyde," said Lady Marblehead. "This is my house. I give the orders."

Mr Melamed would have liked to ask the young man more questions, particularly about the afternoon tea he had taken with Lady Marblehead. If Mr Clyde had eaten the same food and not become ill, then the poison must have been administered at a different time. But when? And how? However, he knew he could not contradict Lady Marblehead's orders, and so the opportunity was lost, for the moment.

After the young man had left the room, Mr Melamed turned to Lady Marblehead and asked, "Milady, I have one last question and then I shall trouble you no more today. What made you engage the services of Mr Taylor? How did you hear about him?"

"That is two questions, sir. But I will answer them both in return for your promise that you will find my bracelet and bring the thief to justice."

"I will try. That is all that I can promise."

"You may rely upon his word," said Mr Powell.

"Then I shall tell you this, Mr Melamed, I did not find Mr Taylor. He found me. A few weeks ago he arrived at my front door with a letter of introduction from some old friends of mine who live in Jamaica. For their sake, I received him. As he seemed to be interested in my ailments and eager to relieve my suffering, I agreed to engage him as my physician. After all that has happened since, I am convinced that that letter must have been a forgery. Indeed, I do not believe that he is a physician, at all. Meat and wine for supper! Who ever heard of such a thing?"

CHAPTER XI

When they were standing on the pavement outside of Lady Marblehead's house, Mr Powell asked, "What do you intend to do now, Melamed?"

"I shall visit the pawnshops and moneylenders. Can you give me a description of the bracelet?"

Mr Powell could and did. He then added, "When Lord Marblehead was still alive they would often go to dinner parties, where Lady Marblehead would show off the bracelet and tell the story about Captain Morgan."

"I was not trying to trick you, when I asked for the description."

Mr Powell shrugged. "I would not have blamed you if you had suspected me. The thought did cross my mind that I would much rather prefer to pawn someone else's jewels than my own."

"Most people would."

"I suppose you can find a way to have Mr Taylor's rooms searched, if the bracelet does not turn up in the usual places."

"I suppose I can. Although I am not entirely convinced that Mr Clyde is as innocent as he would like us to believe. He himself admitted that he knew about the bracelet and where it was hidden. He also had the opportunity to remove the key from Lady

Marblehead's pocket when she was ill and he was alone with her in her bedchamber."

"Should I try to find out if Mr Clyde has made any unexpected expenditures, the sort that a young man would make if he suddenly came into some money?"

"It would help if we had all the facts."

"And what about Jeanette, should we try to locate her?"

"At this point, I think no. Let us first try to find the bracelet. Once it is found, we will know who took it. May I invite you to dine with me this evening?"

"That does not give either one of us much time to make our inquiries."

"No, but if someone really did try to poison Lady Marblehead, we do not want to give our poisoner time to make another attempt on her life."

* * *

Mr Melamed spent a desultory morning going from one pawnbroker to another. No one had in their possession a pearl bracelet that fit the description. None of the moneylenders that he called upon recalled accepting such a bracelet as collateral. But whether the results of his investigation were good or bad for Mr Taylor, he did not know. The bracelet might be hidden in the young man's rooms.

On his way back to Bury Street he passed Devonshire Square and decided to pay a call to Mrs Franks, to see if she had any thoughts about what had caused her daughter's illness. He was surprised to see that both Mr and Mrs Franks were at home and that they were still eating a late breakfast.

"We are feeling a bit under the weather again," Mr Franks explained. "My tailoring customers shall have to do without my services for one day."

"Will you join us?" asked Mrs Franks. "There are scrambled eggs on the buffet, and the rolls should still be warm. There is also coffee, or perhaps you would prefer tea?"

Mr Melamed assured his hosts that he had already breakfasted, but he did accept a cup of tea.

"I hope you will find it acceptable, Mr Melamed," said Mrs Franks. "Our cook purchased a tin from a new tea merchant. I am not fond of the taste, but we are all out of our usual blend." Mrs Franks then turned to her daughter, who was seated by the fire, "Harriet, would you like another cup?"

"No thank you, Mama," said Miss Franks.

Mr Melamed noted that the girl was much changed since he had last seen her. She was paler and thinner, and less animated in her manner.

"I understand that your daughter has been ill for several days," said Mr Melamed. "I trust she is receiving adequate medical care."

Mr and Mrs Franks exchanged glances.

"We have been wondering the same thing ourselves," said Mr Franks. "We called in Mr Taylor when this whole thing began, and he seems to be a very dedicated young man. But since he is still young, it is only natural that he would not have the experience of an older physician."

"You have called in someone else, then?"

"Not another physician," Mr Franks glanced nervously over at his wife. "Mrs Franks thought we should do that, call in old Mr Obadiah. But Rudolph

Ackermann paid us a visit the other day—you remember him, Mr Melamed, do you not?"

"I was leafing through the second volume of *The Microcosm of London* last night. It remains an impressive piece of work."

"He will be pleased to hear you say so. He and Mr Frederick Accum—whom you may also recall—should be here any minute."

"But if neither of these men is a physician ..." Mr Melamed let the question fade away. From the look on the face of Mrs Franks, he correctly surmised that she had raised a similar objection. Since it was possible that an argument had ensued, Mr Melamed thought it best not to add fuel to those marital flames. He therefore took a sip from the cup of tea that Mrs Franks had offered him. She had been correct. It was not a blend that he would have chosen.

"Mr Accum is an excellent chemist," said Mr Franks. "He is doing some very interesting experiments these days, and ..."

Before Mr Franks could say anything more, the butler announced that two gentlemen wished to see Mr Franks. Mr Ackermann, the well-known printer and proprietor of a fashionable art emporium located on the Strand, and Mr Accum, a man of science, entered the room shortly thereafter.

"I have brought a gift for the little girl," said Mr Ackermann, presenting the latest edition of his magazine, *Repository of Arts, Literature, Commerce, Manufactures, Fashion and Politics*, to Mrs Franks, after he had greeted the gentlemen. "I hope she is feeling better."

"You will please excuse her if she does not leave her seat by the fire," said Mrs Franks. "She is still feeling very weak."

"In fact, we are all feeling a little weak this morning," said Mr Franks.

"The illness has returned?" asked Mr Accum.

"A milder case, I hope, but we all had an unhappy night."

Mr Accum glanced from Mr Franks to where Miss Franks was sitting. He then turned his attention to the items that were sitting on the table. "Has your cook been informed that I wish to inspect the contents of her pantry?"

"She has," said Mrs Franks, "but she is not at all happy about it."

"Cooks seldom are," said Mr Accum.

"You suspect that someone may have poisoned the food?" asked Mr Melamed.

"I am a man of science, sir. I proceed methodologically. When a person suffers from a lingering stomach ailment, the natural first place to look is at what is going into that stomach. To first leap to a conclusion that there is a poisoner running loose in the house is bad science."

"I stand corrected, sir," said Mr Melamed, relieved that there was at least one person in the world who seemed not to accuse Mr Taylor of poisoning his patients.

"Mrs Franks, have you prepared for me the list I asked for, the foods that Miss Franks has eaten during the last several days?"

"I have it here, Mr Accum," she replied, removing a page from the embroidered pocket that hung from her gown. "I added the foods that Mr Franks and I ate yesterday, since the illness seems to have returned."

"Good," he said, casting an eye over the page. "I compliment you, Mrs Franks. The list is complete and in excellent order. You, I see, do have the scientific mind. With your permission, I shall proceed to the kitchen."

While Mrs Franks rang for the butler, Mr Melamed said to Mr Franks, "Do you mind if I go with Mr Accum? I feel a certain responsibility, since it was I who asked you to engage Mr Taylor's services."

"I do not see how Mr Accum's inquiry concerns Mr Taylor. Mr Accum is conducting a study of food adulteration. It is a new area of interest for him. He spoke about the topic a few weeks ago, at one of Mr Ackermann's scientific evenings. If you are interested, by all means go with him." Mr Franks then added, "And if you could say a few kind words to our cook about her muffins, perhaps that will soften the blow of having to receive interlopers in her private domain."

It was thus arranged that Mr Ackermann would remain upstairs with the family, and enjoy some of those muffins, while Mr Melamed went with Mr Accum downstairs to the kitchen. Mrs Mattersdorf, who had presided over the kitchen of the Franks family for many long and good years, eyed the two intruders with open hostility. "This is a kosher kitchen, gentlemen," she told them. "I will not allow anyone to mix up the meat knives with the dairy spoons, no matter what the master says."

"I will keep a watchful eye on Mr Accum's movements," Mr Melamed assured her. But apparently that assurance was not enough, since she continued to watch their every gesture like a hawk, a bird that would not normally be allowed in her kosher kitchen.

Mr Accum gave a careful examination of the items stored in the pantry, and then removed a few of the tins and jars, which he placed on the sturdy wood table that stood in the middle of the spacious room. He had brought several of his own containers with him to store samples of food that he would examine later in his chemist's workroom. He was very interested in a collection of jellies that had been sent to the Franks family as a gift. A jar of pickles also was summoned from its place on the shelf and subjected to the knife, which was supplied by the cook. Larger foodstuffs, such as a round of kosher cheese, he ignored completely. He also ignored the remains of a loaf of bread that had been baked in the oven that morning.

"Is there anything in particular you are looking for?" asked Mr Melamed.

"The colour, sir, is what I am looking for - too bright colours that tempt the eye of the ordinary person but trigger in mine suspicion."

"What kind of suspicion?"

"Suspicion that something has been added to the food to make the colour more pleasing to the eye of the customer. I am presently studying copper additives.

"Could that be the cause of Miss Franks's illness?"

"Once more, Mr Melamed, you are too impatient. I am still at the beginning of my experiments."

"But the ingestion of these additives could make a person ill?"

~ 120 ~

"If I did not believe so, I would not be here."

Mr Accum poked his nose into a few other items, and then said to the cook that his inquiry was completed.

While they were climbing up the stairs, Mr Melamed asked if the chemist would mind providing a similar service at the orphanage and, if he could arrange it, at the home of Lady Marblehead. He did not know if she would agree, after the events of the morning, but he thought he would at least make the request.

"I am at your service, sir," replied Mr Accum. "Shall I send you the results of my examination of these samples?"

Mr Melamed said yes, and the two gentlemen went their separate ways.

Mr Melamed's way led him to the orphanage, where he expected to find Mr Taylor. He was unsure how to approach the young man, but he thought the missing bracelet might be the best way to begin. If Mr Taylor was innocent, he might feel insulted by a request to search his rooms, but he would not withhold his permission.

However, instead of finding Mr Taylor he found Miss Taylor, who Mr Melamed discovered sobbing in a courtyard, when he arrived. Although Mr Melamed and his wife had raised two daughters, who were both now happily married, thank G-d, he had never grown used to the sight of a young lady's tears, and so he approached Miss Taylor with some trepidation.

"What is it, Miss Taylor? If I can do anything to help ..."

Miss Taylor gave a frightened start, and then quickly struggled to regain her composure. "Forgive me, Mr Melamed. I am not myself this morning. I suppose you have heard the news."

"No, I have not. What has happened?"

"Earlier this morning there was a meeting of the Jewish Ladies' Charitable Auxiliary; they met in the hall that the Great Synagogue sometimes uses as a tea room. They had asked if my brother would speak to them, about the progress of the children in the orphanage, and he obliged. After the meeting was over, several of the ladies became violently ill and …"

Mr Melamed was not sure if Miss Taylor was about to break into a fresh bout of tears or into a rage. All he knew was that she was struggling with some violent emotion. It was then that he noticed the paper box that she was crushing in her clenched hands.

"What was in this box, Miss Taylor?"

"Sweets, Mr Melamed. My brother had brought them to the meeting, since we are not in the habit of eating such things."

"Did the ladies eat the sweets?"

"Yes. And now people are saying that the candies were poisoned—that my brother deliberately poisoned those ladies, just like he has poisoned the children! And that he dared to commit his crime in the tea room of the Great Synagogue! Oh, Mr Melamed, how can people be so cruel? Do they not know that my brother cannot sleep at night, because he is so worried about those poor orphans?"

"Please try to remain calm, Miss Taylor. Where did your brother get these sweets from?"

"They were in the basket, the one that Miss Lyon brought to us last night."

"Miss Lyon?"

"Yes, she brought us a basket filled with food. She said it was from a grateful community, but we were sure that it was either from her parents, or from you."

"Well, I can assure you that I did not put a box of poisoned sweets in that basket. I shall ask the Lyons if they know anything about the box. In the meantime, where is Mr Taylor now? Is he with the children?"

Miss Taylor hesitated before she answered. "I do not know where he is. But do not think badly of him, Mr Melamed. The accusations—it has been such a shock. And my brother is a sensitive person. He does not show it to others, but he feels things deeply. I am sure he will return to his duties, when he has recovered."

"I understand. And perhaps you should go home, Miss Taylor. It has been a shock for you, as well."

"No, someone has to look after the children." And with that she hurried inside the orphanage.

* * *

Mr Lyon was at home when Mr Melamed called. Although he would normally have been at his fashionable clock-making shop on Cornhill Street at that hour, he had received an urgent summons to return at once to his home in Devonshire Square. Once there, he had been greeted with the distressing news that his helpmeet, Mrs Lyon, who had attended the Jewish Ladies' Charitable Auxiliary meeting earlier, had been taken violently ill and was readying herself to meet her Maker. When he entered the bedchamber, he found Mrs Lyon dictating her ethical will to a trembling Miss Rebecca Lyon.

"Mr Lyon, at last you are here," said the ill lady, who, in truth, was looking a little better, although she was still very weak. "Tell me that you will not forget to provide Rebecca with sewing lessons, after I am gone. I am sure I should have no peace in Heaven if our grandchildren walk about London wearing clothes with ragged hems."

"There, there, my dear," said the family's patriarch, taking his wife's hand. "Surely it is not as bad as you say. It is most likely just a touch of ingestion. Have you summoned Mr Taylor?"

"No!" the good woman cried out, with a strength that almost made Mr Lyon leap from his chair. "It was Mr Taylor that poisoned us! To think that I invited him to our Seder, and put an entire loaf of my gefilte fish into that food basket—such ingratitude I have never seen!"

At this interesting point in the conversation it was announced that Mr Melamed was in the drawing room. Mr Lyon excused himself from his wife's bedside and went to greet the visitor. After Mr Melamed recounted the latest development—news that was substantiated by Mr Lyon, since Mrs Lyon was one of the ladies who had been taken ill—Mr Melamed inquired about the sweets, whose empty box he had brought with him.

"I know nothing about it," said Mr Lyon. "Let me call Rebecca."

When Rebecca arrived in the room, she was informed that Mr Melamed wished to ask her a few questions about the food basket she had delivered to the Taylors on the previous evening. At once she turned very pale, which was noticed by both gentlemen.

"What do you know about the basket, Rebecca?" asked Mr Lyon, before Mr Melamed could phrase his own question. "I see from your face that you do know something."

"Papa, I am sorry. I ... I ... I did not mean to drop it."

Mr Lyon's face was filled with alarm as he had visions of his daughter dropping a tin full of arsenic on the food items in the basket, and then not telling a soul of her error. The powder must have somehow crept into the box of sweets, where it settled, unbeknownst to Mr Taylor or anyone else. The Lyon family would have to escape to the Continent; it would be unthinkable to allow Rebecca to ascend the steps of the gallows. Although she may have inadvertently poisoned a dozen ladies, including her own mother, she was still his daughter. Then he realized that his thoughts were running away with themselves, and he must slow them down. "What ... did ... you ...drop, Rebecca?" he asked, slowly and firmly, in an effort to appear calm.

Rebecca had been following closely the changes in her father's face, and she hoped that he was not going to be ill, too. She therefore replied in kind, as calmly as she could, "The ... basket."

"You dropped the basket?" asked Mr Lyon, having resumed his usual tone of voice.

"Yes."

"Why?" he asked, the only thing he could think of to say while waves of relief were cascading in his mind.

"I did not mean to do it, Papa. But when I tried to give the basket to Miss Taylor, she refused. So I tried again to place it in her hands, and it slipped from my hands and fell to the floor. But they did not seem angry." When her words were met with silence, she glanced from her father to Mr Melamed and asked, "What have I done?"

"You have not done anything wrong, Miss Lyon," said Mr Melamed. "But do you recall there being a box of sweets in the basket?"

Rebecca thought for a moment. "Yes, there was! Hannah's husband bought them, and I remember that I asked Hannah if I could have one. But she said it was for the Taylors, and so she gave me a piece of cake instead."

"Is this the box?" Mr Melamed showed her the box he had received from Miss Taylor.

"I think so, although it looked much nicer last night."

Mr Lyon turned to Mr Melamed and said, "I cannot imagine why my son-in-law would wish to kill off the ladies of our community. If there were no ladies who would there be to buy his jewellery?"

While a wide-eyed Rebecca looked on, the two gentlemen continued to discuss this most interesting situation. Mr Melamed agreed that it was highly unlikely that Mr David Goldsmith, Hannah's husband, would knowingly try to poison the ladies. Indeed, since the food package was meant for Mr Taylor, he, if anyone, should have been the victim of the poisoning attempt.

At this point, Miss Lyon asked for permission to interject a comment, explaining that due to her vast reading of the novels of Mrs Radcliffe, she was something of an expert about poisoners and therefore ...

"Rebecca, how many times have I told you that Mr Melamed does not have time to hear about novels," said Mr Lyon.

"Sometimes a grain of sense can be found within the chaff of imagination," said Mr Melamed. "Let the child talk."

Although Miss Lyon could have protested that she was no longer a child, and that she had left the nursery long ago, she decided to let this comment pass unremarked in order to present the "grain of sense," which in her opinion was actually an entire bushel of sense and not just a single seed. "It seems to me," she began, "that a skilled poisoner would wish to mislead those who were trying to discover his identity. Therefore, he might contrive to send himself a box of poisoned sweets, to show to the world that he was also a victim. But since he would not wish to poison himself, he would give the box to someone else."

"A person might do that," Mr Melamed admitted. "But we know the box came from Mr Goldsmith, who has no connection to the illness that has stricken the children of the orphanage." He then added, "At least no connection that we know of."

"Yes, but how do we know that it was the same box? Perhaps Mr Taylor substituted a box of poisoned sweets for the innocent box that Mr Goldsmith had purchased."

"Or Taylor might have tampered with the box, after he received the basket," Mr Lyon added, still visualizing sprinklings of arsenic in *his* imagination.

Rebecca was pleased that her words were being taken so seriously by her father and Mr Melamed. However, when she recalled that they were not discussing a novel, but a real person—Mr Taylor—her heart sank. She did not know Mr Taylor well, but she was very fond of his sister, and she was distressed on Miss Taylor's account. If it was difficult to find a husband without a dowry, which it was, how would that unfortunate young lady ever find her life's companion once it became known that her brother was a ruthless murderer?

CHAPTER XII

Before Mr Melamed made further inquiries, he decided to return to his rooms on Bury Street. He needed time to sort out his thoughts. But instead of turning into his own building, he stopped at the one next door. He did not truly expect to find Mr Taylor sulking in his rooms and, indeed, no one answered the door when Mr Melamed knocked. He might have forced the lock — he was after all, the owner of the building and the Taylors' landlord. He also reminded himself that he had already stooped very low when he read the letter from Thomas Powell without permission. But something stopped him. Perhaps it was the memory of Miss Taylor's tears, which he felt were genuine. For her sake, he would not yet violate the sanctity of her home. First, he decided, he would arrange for Mr Taylor's laboratory to be searched.

Someone did answer the door, when Mr Melamed knocked on the door below. Master Isaac Goldsmith, who was in his mother's arms, greeted the gentleman cordially. Mrs Hannah Goldsmith also greeted Mr Melamed and invited him to come inside, but he assured her that his business was brief. He showed her the box of sweets, she recognized it, and confirmed that her husband had bought it for the Taylors. She gave Mr Melamed the name of the confectionary shop where she believed her husband had made the purchase.

"Was there anything wrong with the candies?" she asked.

Mr Melamed had no wish to alarm her, but since he was certain that she would hear the news from someone else, if not from him, he told her what he knew. He also reassured her that her mother seemed to be feeling better, and that there was no reason for her to fly to her mother's bedside. Miss Lyon was already sitting there, assuming the duties of a concerned daughter.

When he was sitting in his library, he made a note of the confectioner's name and address. He then noticed that a letter was sitting on his desk. From the foreign address and foreign stamps he correctly assumed that it was a letter from the Chassidic Rebbe that provided spiritual guidance to his daughter and her husband. The letter began as it always did, with respectful greetings and wishes for Mr Melamed's continued good health. This was followed by news about the Jewish community in Bohemia, including news about a few of the charities that Mr Melamed helped to support. Then the Rebbe came to what he called the real business of the letter, an interesting Torah discussion that had taken place at his Seder table.

The days of the Noda B'Yehuda were recalled (the Rebbe wrote), *when there was a plot to poison the first bread that the Jews would eat after the Passover holiday. The great Rabbi, in his wisdom, declared a ninth day of Passover that year, claiming an error in the calendar. The poisoned bread was left uneaten, and the Jews of Prague were saved.*

This incident brought to mind the words of the Rambam, whose medical prowess was as renowned as his insights into our holy Torah. In his time, as well as our more recent days, it seems the poisoner practiced his art without compunction. The Rambam therefore wrote, in his Treatise on Poisons and Their Antidotes, "One does not take any [bread] from those whom he suspects of trickery, but only from those he firmly trusts. It is not far-fetched or difficult to place poison in a simple or complex food and succeed with his intention with any food or beverage taken. Even if it does not kill, it will cause harm and deliverance rests only in the hands of Hashem."

Nine, the letter "tes" in the Holy Tongue, is associated with "tov" (good) and "emes" (truth). This truth can conquer the snake, whose hallmark is trickery and whose tendency is to lie. May Hashem open your eyes to the truth, and may the ninth day see your community restored to good health.

Mr Melamed replaced the letter on his desk. He was not surprised that the Rebbe had seen the London community's current trouble, and it was not because Mr Melamed believed in magic. It had been explained to him once that because a holy person's vision is not cluttered with the mundane things that most people are concerned with—the petty feuds and jealousies, the frivolous amusements and pursuits—that person's vision is clear, unclouded, and therefore able to view what is hidden from the eyes of others.

Yet, as always, it was frustrating that the Rebbe would not provide the solution to the problem in an equally clear fashion. Who, or what, was this snake?

What trickery was creeping its way into the drawing rooms and bedchambers of London's rich and poor, alike?

Mr Melamed took pen and paper, as prelude to an attempt to summarize, in an orderly way, everything that had happened during the past few days. His first impulse was to record only that which had a clear link to the poisonings. Then he recalled his own obscured vision - for he was not so blind as to delude himself that he was a holy person like the Rebbe—and decided to record, instead, all that had occurred during the past several days. Perhaps when all was laid down in black and white, a pattern would emerge from the seemingly unlinked puzzle pieces.

How had it begun? He supposed that it was the Franks family that had first been taken ill. That Accum fellow was busy analysing the contents of their pantry now, so if anything was amiss Mr Melamed should soon find out. If the problem was tainted food bought at some shop, the way was clear. He need only determine if a similar food was found in the pantries of the other afflicted homes.

He was not sure what to write down next, Lady Marblehead's illness or the sickness that had overwhelmed the children at the Jewish orphanage. The two events seemed to have occurred at the same time, if he recalled correctly. But then he recalled that there had been another incident, which had preceded those other events—the incident involving the old clothes man.

Most likely, there was no connection between the visit by the Bow Street Runner and the outbreak of illness that followed, and yet ... At the time, Mr Melamed had found it odd that Mr Powell had entered the conversation and offered the bribe that brought that conversation to a close. Why should he care about an elderly Jewish rag-picker? Was it possible that Mr Powell was in some convoluted way involved with the stolen clothes?

Mr Melamed rested his pen on its holder and shook his head. Once imagination was given its head, where could it not roam? It was ludicrous to think that the worlds of Mr Powell and Mr Schneider, the old clothes man, would ever meet. And yet they had, if only in a roundabout way. What if it were Mr Powell who had taken the bracelet, and deposited it with the old clothes man for safe keeping? He would not want old Jeremiah to divulge that information, in the old man's eagerness to curry the favour of his Bow Street jailer. But had Mr Powell already received the letter from his son at that time? Mr Melamed did not think so; Mr Powell had not seemed worried during their chess game. In fact, he had seemed to be in very good spirits. And he would not have suggested embarking on a business endeavour if he knew he had to pay off his son's gambling debts — unless it had all been a pretense to deflect suspicion from the deed he was about to do.

Mr Melamed dipped his pen into the ink and placed a question mark next to this entry.

The next entry was for Lady Marblehead. The woman had accused her Jewish physician of poisoning her, even before she was aware of the missing bracelet. Her non-Jewish physician had agreed that she had been poisoned, although he did not say by whom. The most likely people to suspect, if indeed the poisoning had been done by a person and not a contaminated food, were Mr Taylor and Mr Clyde.

He decided to confront the problem of Mr Clyde first. The young man would have a motive for poisoning his elderly great-aunt and stealing the bracelet if he were in desperate need of funds. But how could he enter the kitchen of the Franks family, or the orphanage, or the tea room of the Great Synagogue? No, if he indeed was involved with all that—again, perhaps to deflect suspicion from his true intended crime—he would need an accomplice. He would need the help of someone who was familiar with the Jewish community and who had the means to accomplish the nefarious scheme.

Mr Melamed stopped, with pen in mid-air. The conversation in the corridor outside Lady Marblehead's bedchamber came back to him, vividly. He had mentioned to Mr Powell that the Jewish physician had grown up in Jamaica. Then Mr Clyde had left the sick room in a hurry, and Mr Powell had looked after the young man and said, "I wonder."

"I wonder," Mr Melamed repeated softly. Mr Clyde was also from Jamaica. Had he known Gabriel Taylor? Was Taylor somehow in the young man's debt? Or did the two men both have their eye on Lady Marblehead's fortune?

Yet if the two young men were working together, why had Mr Clyde so openly tried to place the blame at Mr Taylor's door? Had the discovery of the stolen bracelet unnerved him? And why had only the bracelet been stolen, and not the entire contents of the box? Was it meant to be a first payment to Mr Taylor, for his part in the plot? Or had Mr Clyde taken the bracelet for his own use, perhaps to pay off some pressing debts that could not be put off, but was content to wait for the rest after Lady Marblehead's death?

But would there have been time to convince Lady Marblehead to make a new will before the poisoning attempt, one in Mr Clyde's favour? Mr Melamed thought not, yet stranger things had happened. He must somehow find out if a new will had been drawn up, and if there was a connection between Mr Taylor and Mr Clyde and, of course, if the pearl bracelet was in Mr Taylor's rooms. Any of those tasks would take considerable time, if he tried to accomplish them alone. Fortunately, though, he knew of a way to shorten the path and despite his hesitation to sink even further into the mire, he knew he had no choice but to take it. Whether the poisoning was intentional or not, too many people were becoming much too ill—and it had to be stopped.

* * *

General Well'ngone pulled out a watch from his great coat's pocket. Whether or not the watch was an accurate predictor of the hour was anyone's guess, but he studied the face with great interest before he snapped the cover shut and said, "I hope you are not expecting to be invited to tea, Mr Melamed. This is not the hour when the Earl is accustomed to dine."

"It is not my accustomed hour to dine either, General," Mr Melamed replied. And in truth, even if it were an hour when Mr Melamed was accustomed to partake of some light refreshments, he would not have done so at the Earl's table. He knew very well that the Earl and his boys had little to eat, and that this little would not be attractive to his more refined palate.

With those preliminaries concluded, General Well'ngone allowed the visitor entry to the Earl's residence on Gravel Lane. A handful of young urchins followed the General and Mr Melamed down the dimly lit stairs, but the children were not granted admittance to the Earl's inner sanctum.

It took a few minutes for Mr Melamed to accustom himself to the smell of dampness that pervaded the room. He did note that the Earl was wearing a new waistcoat – or, rather, one that was new for the Earl. Once, perhaps twenty years previous, the waistcoat must have been stunning. But with the passage of time the brilliance of most of the coloured threads had faded. Only here and there could a glimpse of brilliant scarlet or dazzling sapphire-blue be seen, a slim remembrance of the splendour and glory of a former age, which had since passed from the stage of life and settled into dust.

Mr Melamed further noted that the Earl had recently powdered his wig, another affectation of the Earl, who styled himself after an eighteenth-century gentleman, presumably because those cast-off fashions could be more easily retrieved from the dustbins of London than the more sombre coats and waistcoats that characterized the present age.

The Earl removed his quizzing glass from his waistcoat pocket and put it to his eye. "I am happy to see that the plague has not reached as far as Bury Street, Mr Melamed. You look well. But, you always do. My compliments to your tailor." He then paused and struck a more commanding pose, before continuing, "It is a Taylor that you have come about, is that not so, Mr Melamed?"

"As always, Earl, your intelligence is excellent."

The Earl allowed himself a slight smile of satisfaction and gestured, graciously, for his visitor to take a seat. Mr Melamed sat, inwardly thankful that the dirty fabric seemed to be reasonably dry. Yet even more distasteful than the room and its furnishings — a person could not help it if he was poor and could afford no better — was the person who inhabited that room, in Mr Melamed's opinion. He despised the Earl, who had more than once been invited to turn his hand to a more honest and respectable way to earn his daily bread, and each time the Earl had refused the offer. The Earl preferred to be the king of the pickpockets who lived on Gravel Lane, than to be an anonymous labourer in Mr Lyon's clock-making workshop or a similar establishment engaged in weaving or candle-making.

Yet ever since Mr Melamed took on the role of investigator of crimes that affected London's Jewish community, he found himself forced to turn to the Earl for assistance. The Earl and his boys, who had the trick of seemingly knowing everyone while remaining invisible to all, were able to ferret out information that Mr Melamed would never have been able to lay his hand upon. Mr Melamed therefore overcame his distaste and said, "What exactly do you know about Mr Taylor?"

"You understand, of course, I cannot divulge how I obtained my information."

"Believe me, Earl, I have no wish to interest myself in your affairs more than I must."

"I do believe you, sir. And because I believe I owe you a small favour concerning an old clothes man named Jeremiah Schneider, I will tell you that I know that the boys at the orphanage do not suspect that Mr Taylor is poisoning them. But there are certain people who suspect that he was involved in the attempt to poison Lady Marblehead."

Mr Melamed knew he should not be surprised that the Earl's web spread as far as Mayfair, but he was. Yet this made his request easier to accomplish, he hoped. "Do these people, the ones who suspect Mr Taylor, suspect that he acted alone, or was someone else also involved?"

"Really, Mr Melamed," General Well'ngone chimed in, "if you suspect your friend Mr Powell wanted to send his relative off to Heaven before she was ready, why don't you ask him yourself and not waste the Earl's time?"

"I was actually referring to Mr Clyde. He is Lady Marblehead's great-nephew, and recently arrived from Jamaica."

"You interest me, Mr Melamed," said the Earl. "Have you a raindrop in this bet?"

Mr Melamed glared at the young man. "What on earth are you talking about?"

"Ask your friend, Mr Powell. I believe the charmingly idiotic pastime of betting on raindrops began in his gentlemen's club. I hear it has been replaced, though, in popularity by a wager concerning who poisoned Lady Marblehead. If you are placing your bet on Mr Clyde, you must have a reason."

"I am not in the habit of placing bets, and certainly not when the stakes are a man's life. What I want your boys to find out is if Mr Clyde is in communication with Mr Taylor."

"You think the two of them are in cahoots?" exclaimed the General, his interest piqued by this unexpected development.

"You have a quick wit, General," said Mr Melamed. "It is a pity you have chosen to waste it."

"Have you considered, Mr Melamed, that it is our profession which has sharpened those brains that you seem to admire?" asked the Earl. "But we digress, and descend to the level of the petty squabble, which does credit to neither of us. If I have understood you correctly, you have no real reason to suspect Mr Clyde, other than that he is young, probably in need of money, and therefore impatient for the old lady to die."

"That is, in a general way, correct."

"You therefore wish us to keep an eye on Mr Taylor and Mr Clyde. Agreed. Is there anything else?"

"Yes, two more things. I wish to know who inherits under Lady Marblehead's will. I assume that Mr Powell and his son will inherit something. But I wish to know if Mr Clyde will receive monies or property, and how much. Is that something your boys can find out?"

If there had been more candles in the room, Mr Melamed might have seen a flicker of light momentarily brighten the Earl's eye. But all he saw was the half bow that the Earl made as he said, "We are at your service, Mr Melamed. The third request?"

"I have let a room in the back of Mr Taylor's apartments on Bury Street. Mr Taylor uses it as a laboratory to conduct scientific experiments, which he sometimes does late at night, after he has completed his other duties and dined. The room has a window. I would like one or two of your boys to observe what Mr Taylor does when he is in that room."

"One minute, Mr Melamed," said the General, "how should we know a thing like that? Our boys aren't doctors and murderers."

"I do not expect you to understand the nature of his experiments. Just observe his actions. And observe if he is alone, or not."

Mr Melamed placed several sovereigns on the table. "Buy your boys a good dinner, Earl," he said, rising from his chair. "There will be more of these after they make their report." Mr Melamed was almost at the door when he stopped, turned back to the Earl and said in what he hoped sounded like an unconcerned tone of voice, "There is one more thing you might do for me, Earl. A pearl bracelet has gone missing from Lady Marblehead's jewellery box. If you should find it in any of the places you will be visiting, and you might want to pay a call to Jeremiah Schneider's rooms, as well, bring the bracelet to me. I will pay you better than any pawnbroker, I promise."

When the General had returned, after escorting Mr Melamed back up the stairs and to the street, he plopped down on the recently vacated chair and said, "Who do you think pinched that bracelet?"

"I do not care. Just make sure you find it."

"And how are we supposed to find out about that will?"

"If you don't know the answer to that, it must be because you have left those wits that Mr Melamed so much admired in that gentleman's pocket," replied

the Earl with a smile. "But have no fear, before this
night is over, you shall see how to fish them out."

CHAPTER XIII

Mr Powell's morning had been more productive than Mr Melamed's visits to the pawnshops. He had discovered that Mr Clyde had paid a visit to a first-rate tailor on Bond Street, made inquiries at Tattersall's concerning a horse, and lost a modest sum of money at a gaming establishment. Further prodding had revealed that Mr Clyde had paid a visit to a pawnshop, but it was a diamond and pearl ring that he had pawned to pay for his expenditures, and not a pearl bracelet.

"That is why you did not discover it," said Mr Powell, while he was dining with Mr Melamed. "It is very possible that the ring was his, you know. My cousin did not mention that she had missed it."

Mr Melamed did not tell his friend about his visit to the Earl of Gravel Lane, but he did mention his visit to the Franks home and his meeting Mr Accum. "I thought it might be worthwhile to have Mr Accum inspect the contents of Lady Marblehead's pantry, as well."

"I can understand why you would prefer to discover that Mr Taylor is innocent, but I find it hard to believe that a contaminated jelly or pickle is the real culprit. Still, I suppose there is no harm in asking my cousin. Frankly, it will probably be amusing to see her reaction."

Mr Powell was not disappointed, when he and Mr Melamed returned to Mayfair after they had dined.

"A pickle?!" Lady Marblehead spat out, after Mr Powell explained about Mr Accum's latest area of scientific inquiry and asked if that gentleman could receive permission to study the contents of the Mayfair residence's pantry. "Are you suggesting that it was a pickle that made off with my pearl bracelet, as well?!"

"An interesting idea, ma'am; I had not thought of it. But returning to the subject of your late illness, if it was not a pickle …"

"You both must be mad. I do not eat pickles!"

"It might have been caused by a box of candies," said Mr Melamed. "Do you recall eating any sweets before you became ill?"

"How should I remember, Mr Melamed, when I have been to death's door and back only a few days ago? I assure you that such a journey makes a Channel crossing seem like heaven." To prove her point, Lady Marblehead sank back into her pillows and closed her eyes.

"But have you an objection to permitting Mr Accum inside your home?" Mr Powell persisted.

"I should not wish to hinder science. Lord Marblehead was always very interested in science. He was a member of several scientific associations, if you will recall. Just be sure to lock up the silver before that chemist of yours arrives. I have no interest in being robbed a second time."

* * *

It was already evening when Mr Melamed found the time to pay a visit to the confectionary shop. While his carriage wended its way through London's still busy streets he saw the panoply of that great city's life pass by his carriage window like scenes from a magic lantern. There was the peddler, carrying his tattered wares in a wooden box that hung from his neck like a donkey's halter; two soldiers, spruce in their new uniforms, strode through the crowd, pretending not to see the admiring glances of the milliners' assistants, who eagerly gulped in the cool evening air after having been cooped up in their thread-and-needle attic all day. An elderly man, still straight of back and careful of dress—a banker, perhaps, or a solicitor—marched forward, confident that the swelling crowd of clerks, beggars, and messenger boys would part before him, like the humble waves give way to the mighty prow of one of His Majesty's ships, and they did.

It was a show that could be seen on almost any night, although each night the magic-lantern-like scene must change. One day the elderly banker would sit at his great desk no more, the milliner girl would marry, the soldier would return home scarred and weary, if he returned at all. But they would be replaced by others, eager to take part in this nightly parade that Mr Melamed viewed with a melancholy eye. For somewhere within that seemingly innocent promenade was a snake dressed in a man's clothes—and his part, for he knew that he was also part of the scene, was to charm that snake into casting off his lying mask.

His reverie was interrupted by the sight of the confectionary shop, which was easy to spot. A crowd of poor children stood on the street, staring into the shop's brightly lit window. The sweets—a dazzling rainbow of colours, each colour promising a taste of paradise—held their rapt attention. Inside, a lady and gentleman were making their selection. When they were through, Mr Melamed made his. He cared not how the pretty candies tasted; his purpose, instead, was to collect a variety of samples for Mr Accum to examine.

When his business was concluded, he instructed his coachman to drive to the chemist's rooms. On the way there, Mr Melamed thought he spotted two of the Earl's boys. Normally, he would have not wished them success, because he knew that they were usually up to no good. But since it was possible that they were engaged on his mission, he did wish them well as they disappeared into one of London's many dimly lit alleyways.

* * *

"Psst! Over here!" General Well'ngone stayed pressed against the brick wall, as he beckoned to the two boys who had just arrived.

"Ouch!" one of them muttered, having twisted his foot in the uneven paving stones.

"Silence," the General ordered in a whisper, and then pulled them even closer when the two boys had come near. "Hyman, Saulty, up there is the window. Do you see it, lads? Nod your heads, if you do."

Hyman and Saulty nodded.

"Saulty, you be the look-out. Hyman, when I throw down a box, you be there to catch it. Understand?"

~ 145 ~

Again the two boys nodded.

"If someone comes, curl up on the pavement and pretend this alleyway is your bed for the night."

Instead of nodding, Hyman asked, "What do I do after I catch the box, General? Do I run, or do I wait for you to jump down?"

"Neither." General Well'ngone then revealed a peddler's box, which he had borrowed for the night's purpose. "You'll put the box underneath this display of sewing things and trinkets. Here's a cloth to put over the box, so no one will see it. Then you'll walk slow and easy until the quarter bell tolls. From there, grab a carriage and fly to Gravel Lane."

The General put a coin in the boy's pocket, to pay for the carriage. To Saulty he said, "We'll travel together."

General Well'ngone had never trained for the circus, and so his agility must have been due to some natural talent given to him by Hashem. In just a few minutes he reached the open window, and with seemingly no effort at all swung his youthful limbs into Mr Waters' unguarded room. There was little light, but the General needed only a little, used as he was to darkness. To his satisfaction he saw that the box had been left where Mr Waters had said it would be—a black ribbon tied thrice around the case was the previously agreed upon signal. In practically no time the box was tossed, caught, and hidden.

The General waited until after Hyman had sauntered back to the main street, before he climbed down from his window-sill perch. When he was back upon the ground, he cast a last glance at the window, which was still open, as they had arranged with Mr

~ 146 ~

Waters. The job had gone well, yet for some reason that made the General uneasy.

"What's wrong?" asked Saulty, who was eager to be on his way.

"Nothing," replied General Well'ngone. "I hope."

* * *

The Earl sat at the head of the table, listening to the General's report. Hyman and Saulty had been dismissed to what served as the kitchen, where they were eating their evening meal. The box's black ribbon had been removed, and the Earl glanced at the papers while he listened. He had not been given permission to examine the box's contents — his orders from Waters had been to hide the box and everything in it, until the Earl received further instructions — but he assumed that Waters must know that he would take a look inside; he also assumed that since Waters knew that neither the Earl nor anyone under his command could read well enough to understand legal missives, that the Earl's looking through the papers would be a worthless endeavour.

General Well'ngone, having finished speaking, also cast his eye upon the pages. "That's a box full of verbiage, if I've ever seen one. I wonder why Waters didn't just burn the pages, if he doesn't want them."

"We must find someone who can read, General. I must know if one of these verbiages, as you call them, is a will."

"Why not give the box to Mr Melamed? He can read."

~ 147 ~

"Not yet. First, I want to know what this box contains. Who else among our circle of friends is familiar with the art of deciphering scribbles?"

The General thought for a moment. He knew that Simon was teaching himself to read, but he presumed that the boy was still too new to the world of letters to be able to comprehend a legal missive. He needed someone older, someone who was used to sitting by a candle, without caring that the wax dripped on his hand. That thought led him naturally to, "What about old Jeremiah?"

When the Earl looked doubtful, the General continued, "That's all he ever does of a night, sits by his candle, with a book before him, mumbling to himself, and turning the pages. If that's not reading, what is? And while he's here inhaling this dried ink, one of our boys can have a look around his place of abode."

Old Jeremiah was duly summoned, and the task was explained. "I can try, gentlemen, I can only try. But I was never a lawyer's clerk. The words may be unfamiliar to me."

"We only want the will, if it is there," said the Earl. "The rest you can ignore."

"Just sit yourself here, Jeremiah," said the General. "And if you need another candle …"

The General looked over to the Earl, who said, with his usual magnanimity, "We'll somehow procure one."

If there had been a clock in the Earl's drawing room, it would have ticked and tocked its way around the numbered oval until a full hour had passed and fled. But since there was not, time was marked by the shrinking of the candle, which still

~ 148 ~

had some service in it when Jeremiah finally looked up and said, "I cannot say that I have understood every word, but even with all the "by your leaves" and "heretofores" I have a fair idea of what this will says."

The Earl gestured for the old clothes man to continue.

"The bulk of the estate goes to a gentleman named Powell."

"Arthur Powell?"

Jeremiah glanced back down at the document in question. "No, it's a young gentleman that's mentioned, Thomas Powell."

"That must be Mr Powell's son," said the General.

"Is a Mr Clyde mentioned?" asked the Earl.

"Yes, he is," said Jeremiah, marking with his thumb the place on the page where that name appeared. "But he does not get much, poor lad. It seems he never wrote to his great-aunt or sent her presents."

The General tut-tutted and said, "Youth! What's the world coming to?"

The General might have continued along this vein, but the Earl stopped him and said to Jeremiah, "Is there anything else of interest in the will?"

"Only a few small legacies to her servants, a butler named Smithern and her cook."

"You are sure there is nothing for Mr Arthur Powell?"

Jeremiah laboriously perused the document again. "Here's something, Earl. Arthur Powell gets Lord Marblehead's collection of daggers from India."

"It looks like he didn't give the old lady presents, either," said the General.

"I wouldn't be so quick to dismiss the gift," said Jeremiah. "Some of those Indian cut-throaters have handles that are all bejewelled. I've seen one that, were it mine to sell, would turn me into a gentleman with a country house and carriage and four."

They were all silent for a moment. Then the Earl said, "Thank you, Jeremiah. Go down to the kitchen and ask the boys to pour you a glass of ale." The Earl also put one of Mr Melamed's coins on the table, for remuneration. "But don't go home yet. I may need your services for another small job."

After the boy sent to search Jeremiah's room had returned and reported that no pearl bracelet had been found, the old clothes man was once again summoned to the Earl's drawing room.

"Jeremiah, it is important that I keep these papers, but I cannot keep them here; they might be discovered by the wrong persons. I must therefore ask you to hide them for a few days."

"Where can I hide them? What if I'm caught?"

"Say you found the box lying in some alleyway and took it home. It is a nice box, is it not? I can think of several uses for it, don't you agree, General Well'ngone?"

"I'd say it's a perfect box for storing handkerchiefs, Earl, especially ones that are embroidered with a W and a J. What do you say, Jeremiah?"

"I say I didn't say where I got that handkerchief from. I told that to you, General, and now I'm telling it again to you, Earl. It wasn't me that squawked. I don't know how that Bow Street Runner traced it back to your door."

"Calm yourself, Jeremiah," said the Earl. "I'm ready to forget the incident and never mention the handkerchief again, if you will do me this favour."

Jeremiah took the box reluctantly. When the Earl and the General were once again alone, Well'ngone blurted out the question that had been bothering him for some time, "Why didn't Waters burn those papers, if he doesn't want them?"

"Apparently he can't, for some reason," replied the Earl. "It must be that something has frightened him—the attempt to poison Lady Marblehead, most likely—and so he doesn't want the papers in his office, at least not now."

"What's that got to do with Waters? He's a solicitor, not a physician."

"True, but what happens after a doctor's services are no longer needed?"

"The family starts looking for the will."

"And what if the will cannot be found?"

"They throttle the lawyer."

"Unless the solicitor raises a hue and cry: 'Zounds! I've been robbed!'"

"But why doesn't Waters want the will to be found? Do you think there's something fishy about it?"

"Possibly. But I do wonder what would happen if the will was temporarily lost, say long enough to distribute Lady Marblehead's property after she dies. Who would get her money?"

"Her next of kin, isn't that the way the law works?"

"And who is that?"

"If this Mr Clyde is a great-nephew, he's related to the old lady by blood. So I suppose that makes him

~ 151 ~

a closer relation than Powell & Son, who are related only through marriage, according to what the will said."

"Exactly."

"You mean, then, that if there were no will, Mr Clyde would inherit everything?"

"It seems that way, given my limited and rather specialized knowledge of the law.

"Now that's a lovely picture you're painting," said General Well'ngone, his eyes lit up with understanding. "Do you think it was Clyde who paid Waters to hire us to pinch the will?"

"It's a possibility."

"I wouldn't mind getting our hands on a piece of that inheritance—maybe one of them Indian daggers—seeing it's us who have the will. We could threaten the two of them that we're going to expose the plot to Mr Melamed and Mr Powell, if they don't share the spoils."

"Not yet, we can't. For one thing, the lady is still alive, so no one gets anything. For another thing, we don't know for a certainty the real reason why Waters was so eager to make this will disappear. Mr Clyde may have had nothing to do with it. And the third thing …"

The Earl looked momentarily puzzled. "What was it that Waters told you? If he goes to the gallows, he's bringing Taylor with him?"

"That's right."

"The third thing is, where does Mr Taylor come into all this?"

"Do you think that water rat intends to use Mr Taylor as a hostage, so we won't tell the law that he asked us to steal the will? He probably knows that we wouldn't let a fellow Jew go to the gallows."

"It's possible, if Waters does know something that he could use to connect Mr Taylor to these poisonings."

"I am shocked, Earl. I am genuinely shocked. Imagine, a respectable solicitor like Mr Waters turning the tables and trying to blackmail us. This is going beyond all the bounds of decency. But we're not going to let him get away with it, are we?"

The Earl smiled. "Heavens, no."

CHAPTER XIV

Mr Taylor was not sure how long he had been walking through the streets of London. He supposed he was a coward for not returning to the orphanage and facing the charges that had been in hurled in his face. He knew it was not fair to leave Elisheva to face them alone. But every time he tried to direct his steps back toward the orphanage some invisible force seemed to turn him about and push him in a different way.

Finally, his steps led him toward the old Jewish cemetery on Alderney Road. It was not the most cheerful spot in the world, but through the open gate he could see a stone bench in the distance, a sight that brought to the foreground of his still confused thoughts his extreme weariness. He entered, and as he walked he passed by the silent graves of distinguished members of London's Jewish community of days gone by. There was the final resting place of Rabbi David Schiff, a former Chief Rabbi of London. He also passed by the grave of Rabbi Samuel Falk, a Kabbalist who was known as the Baal Shem Tov of London and was thought, during his lifetime, to have had miraculous powers.

If Mr Taylor had been inclined to spirituality and mysticism, he might have stopped at the grave of Rabbi Falk to say a prayer to the One Above for assistance; it is thought by some that the grave site of a righteous person is an auspicious place to offer up such prayers. But Mr Taylor, although believing in the truth of the Torah, was a man of science and he did not give much credence to so-called miracle workers. He believed that, with the help of Hashem, a person should be able to solve a problem using his own intelligence.

Perhaps that is why he sank down upon the bench with so much weariness. For hours he had tried to wrestle with the stubborn problem whose solution had eluded that intelligence, but he was beaten. The only remedy he could find, now that his name had been linked to the poisoning attacks in the orphanage, the tea room, and Lady Marblehead's residence, was to resign his position at once.

But where would he go, what would he do? His only training was in the medical arts. What community would hire him, once it was discovered that his name had been linked to these poisoning cases?

No, there were only two paths open to him. One was to join those who surrounded him, the souls who were sleeping in the ground. The other …

* * *

"What the …!"

"What's wrong?"

"He gave me a fright."

"Who?"

"That man, the one sitting over there on that bench."

The two gravediggers looked over to where Mr Taylor was sitting. Earlier they had set a tombstone into its place, and then gone into their shed to clean and store their tools. Now they were ready to go home.

"We must tell him we're locking up the front gate," said one of the men.

"You do it," said the other one. "I'll have a look around to make sure no one else snuck in while we were in the shed."

When he reached the bench and saw the man's face, the Jewish gravedigger tipped his cap and said, "Begging your pardon, Mr Taylor, but we're getting ready to lock the cemetery for the night."

Mr Taylor stared at the man for a moment before rising from his seat. He gave one last lingering glance around the House of Eternity, as though loathing to leave the tranquil realm, and then said, more to himself than anyone else, "I suppose it is the other path, then."

* * *

By the time Mr Taylor reached Bury Street, pangs of hunger had recalled him to the very real cares of this world, for as almost anyone will tell you, it is extremely difficult to think upon such profound matters as Eternity on an empty stomach. But before he could reach his door, he was stopped by a young boy.

"Please, sir, my foot is hurting me again something bad."

Mr Taylor did not know who the child was; he was not one of the orphanage's boys. The orphanage was too small to contain all the abandoned children who begged or stole for their daily bread and made a stone step their nightly bed. One evening he had seen the child limping badly and brought the boy to his room in the back of Bury Street. He had cleaned the wound and bandaged it. He had also told the child to rest in bed for several days, to allow the wound to heal. They both knew that was impossible. How was the child to eat? Where would he find food, even if he had a bed to rest in?

"I will take a look," said Mr Taylor, and he led the child through the alleyway.

When they reached the room that Mr Taylor used as his laboratory, he helped the boy onto the table, since the room had neither bed nor sofa. "It may hurt when I remove the bandage. Have you eaten supper yet?"

"No, sir."

"You shall have some with me, afterward." Mr Taylor then began to talk of the food that they would presently enjoy together, hoping that such pleasant thoughts would dull the pain of the examination.

Meanwhile, General Well'ngone and Saulty had crept into the alley and noiselessly hurried to the lighted window, which was too high up to offer a full view of the room inside.

"You shall have to be my footstool," whispered the General.

Saulty bent down, so that Well'ngone could climb onto his shoulders. From that perch, the General had a partial view of the room and he could see the head and shoulders of Mr Taylor walking about. But just as he was getting settled into a comfortable position, a scream from inside the room almost made the General lose his balance and tumble to the ground.

"What was that?" whispered Saulty.

"Ssshh!"

General Well'ngone strained his neck to get a better view. He saw Mr Taylor go over to the far side of the room and remove a box from the top shelf of a cabinet. Several moments later he saw the glint of a knife and after that came a second piercing scream.

"He's killing someone in there!" Saulty whispered. "What'll we do?"

Before the General could reply, they heard footsteps approaching. The General quickly jumped down and the two boys took cover. When the person drew near, General Well'ngone almost let out a whistle of surprise.

The person looked around him and behind him before knocking softly on the door. Mr Taylor called out, "Come in," and the man quickly did so. The General just as quickly signalled to Saulty to get back into his previous position.

Mr Taylor greeted his visitor and asked him to be seated in the only comfortable chair in the room. "Thank you, Gabriel, you're a good lad," said old Jeremiah as he placed his heavy bundle on the ground and his weary bones into the seat. "What's wrong with the child?"

"I had to give him a sedative. His foot is badly infected. The pain was too much."

"He can't hear us, then?"

"No."

"You look tired, Gabriel."

"I suppose I am. It has been a long day."

~ 158 ~

"Time is always long when a person is in trouble."

"You have heard what happened this morning?"

"Who has not?"

"Is the law looking for me?"

"Not yet, from what I hear. But Mr Melamed is. You will have to speak with him some time, unless you are thinking of hopping over to the Continent, or back to Jamaica."

"I must finish cleaning this wound. You will excuse me, I hope, if I devote my full concentration to the task."

The old man watched the young man work for a few minutes, and then he said, "I am sorry to bother you again, Gabriel, when you are having so many troubles of your own."

"If I can be of service, sir," the physician wearily replied.

"I hope you can, because I have nowhere else to turn. I need to hide a box. It's only for a few days."

"May I ask what is inside the box?"

Jeremiah slowly removed the box, which he had hidden inside his coat. "It is probably better if you do not know. Cannot you just say that you accepted the box as payment for some treatment you did for someone—someone who came to you from off the street, like this boy? That is, if your room is searched and the box is found."

Having finished with cleaning the wound, Mr Taylor proceeded to bandage the child's foot with a fresh piece of linen. "I am sorry, sir, but I cannot do it. I am already halfway to the gallows, myself, as you well know."

"Do not say it, boy, not even in jest. You must keep up your courage, no matter what other people are saying. But I understand, and perhaps you are right. It would not do if someone were to search your rooms concerning this poisoning matter and find these papers, too. I just wish I could think of a place to keep them, some place that no one would look."

"I was in Alderney Cemetery today. Why don't you bury them there?"

Jeremiah's face, which had been gloomy until then, brightened up. "That's an idea, that is. I always knew you had a good head. Have you any old sheets I can use to wrap around the box, to protect it a bit?"

Mr Taylor had only one to spare, which he handed to the old clothes man. "Will you join me for supper, sir?"

"Thank ye, but I have already dined. And I want to take care of this errand right away. I wouldn't mind, though, a taste of something to warm up my bones before I go."

Mr Taylor returned to the cabinet, where he stored kosher brandy, which was sometimes needed to revive a patient. But when he reached for a cup that was sitting on the top shelf, his hand felt a strange object sitting where the cup should have been.

"What is this?" he said, as he brought the object over to the light.

* * *

The General was not able to hear the conversation that was taking place inside the room, since the window was shut. And even though his vision was

~ 160 ~

partly obscured, he could see just enough to almost lose his balance a second time that night.

"The bracelet!" he almost shouted, but he remembered the necessity for silence in time. Instead, he did whisper to his companion, "Stand up straighter, Saulty! I've got to see what Taylor does next."

Saulty tried to grow another inch or two, and General Well'ngone did the same, as well. The increased height allowed the General to see Mr Taylor give the bracelet to Jeremiah. Having seen that much, General Well'ngone decided that he had seen enough, because he correctly assumed that Jeremiah would soon be departing.

"Be ready to follow the old man," General Well'ngone whispered to his companion, after they had once again taken cover.

A few minutes later the door opened and Jeremiah, looking this way and that as he went, quickly made his way toward Bury Street.

General Well'ngone took a few steps forward, but when he noticed that Saulty wasn't following him he turned back.

"I'm not going," said Saulty.

"What's wrong with you?"

"What's in that bundle that Jeremiah's carrying, that's what I want to know?"

"A bracelet - and we're going to see where old Jeremiah hides it."

"What does he need a bundle that big for, if it's just a bracelet?"

"What are you trying to say, Saulty?"

"I'm saying there's a dead boy wrapped up in that bundle of old rags. I bet that sawbones is a

~ 161 ~

maniac and he snatches boys and cuts 'em all up for his medical experiments."

"You have rats in your attic."

"Do I? And do you hear anyone screaming in that room anymore?"

The General turned and listened. It was true, the room was deathly quiet. "Come on, or we'll lose him," he said, as he hurried to follow the old man.

* * *

General Well'ngone should not have been surprised when the gate to the Jewish cemetery on Alderney Road loomed up before him, for they had been walking in that direction for some time. But when he saw Jeremiah toss the bundle over the high brick wall and then scramble up that same wall after it, he gave a shudder. He knew it was pointless to ask Saulty to accompany him inside; the boy was already looking pale as a ghost and it would be no help if Saulty fainted at the sight of the moonlight playing tricks with the tombstones. The General therefore instructed Saulty to keep watch; he would follow Jeremiah over the wall and enter the cemetery alone.

Reader, I could write that the graveyard was silent as the grave—but how can I know that this is true? A grave, we know is silent. But perhaps, on that troubled night, some bird sang out a few notes of a mournful tune. Perhaps a leaf or two rustled softly in the wind. Perhaps, but we shall never know. What I can tell you is that the hearts of both Jeremiah and the General were beating so loudly that they could scarce hear anything else, not even their muffled footsteps—muffled because each took care not to make a sound.

Jeremiah seemed to know where a spade could be found, because he darted into a crumbling stone structure and emerged with the tool in his hand. Then he stopped to consider where to dig, finally choosing a lonely spot by the far wall. As this was an area where no graves were, and therefore no gravestones to provide cover, the General could approach no further. He remained where he was, hidden behind a tree whose hoary limbs had waved a last goodbye to who knew how many Jewish souls, until the old clothes man had finished with his ghastly work.

How long did that take? In old Jeremiah's opinion, it must have taken a good half hour or so, since he was old and the ground was hard and he was not used to such hard physical work. But were a person to ask General Well'ngone, he would have said that he spent half the night hidden behind that tree.

At last, Jeremiah was satisfied that his handiwork was good enough to escape detection. He returned the spade and left the cemetery as he had entered it, by scrambling over the brick wall as best as his old bones would carry him.

General Well'ngone waited for a few minutes, while he considered what to do: dig up the bracelet, or leave it undisturbed and instead report its location to the Earl. Some mournful sound — perhaps the hooting of some nocturnal bird — made the decision for him. In an instant the fear that he had kept bottled up inside burst forth. In his rush to bid adieu to the moon-washed tombstones that stood like silent watchman guarding an eternal night, he tripped over a gravestone that was shorter in height than the

~ 163 ~

others and obscured by the overgrown ground. If he had not been in such a hurry, he might have seen a timely reminder of man's mortality staring back at him from the stone protrusion; for engraved on the sarcophagus, contrary to Jewish custom, was a blank-eyed, grinning skull. But General Well'ngone was in a hurry. He ran to the wall, found a foothold to help him to the top, and jumped down on the other side.

Even though Saulty's bravery had failed the boy at a crucial moment, General Well'ngone did not care a bit when he saw his companion shivering in the distance. He could have hugged the boy, just because Saulty was alive, and he was alive, and there was a high brick wall separating his London from the London of the dead. But because he did not wish to let on that he had been terrified during his ghostly vigil, he merely said, "I hope the boys didn't eat all the cheese. My stomach is empty as a grave-robbered tomb."

CHAPTER XV

Although General Well'ngone was by then familiar with the alleyway that ran behind Bury Street, he was less familiar with entering a Bury Street residence through the front door. But, as usual, he tried his best not to show it when Mr Melamed's butler answered the rap of the door knocker and opened the door for the General and Saulty.

"Don't wipe your nose with your sleeve," whispered Well'ngone, as the two followed the butler down the long hall. "Haven't you got a handkerchief?"

Saulty did not and he was about to see if the butler had a spare one in his back pocket, when General Well'ngone stopped the boy's hand before the deed could be done.

Mr Melamed was waiting for the two boys in the library — he was not about to let them run loose in his rooms and there was an awkward moment while he hesitated to invite them to sit down, clothed as they were in their filthy, ragged clothes. In the end, hospitality won out over concerns about the upholstery and the two boys took a seat on the sofa. Refreshments were brought in, but General Well'ngone, keenly aware of his duty, said that he would not taste a morsel until he had given his report.

"Where shall we begin?" asked Mr Melamed.

Before the General could reply, there was a loud pounding on the front door and, when the door was opened, a roar of raised voices. The next minute the door to the library was flung open, despite the protestations of Mr Melamed's butler, and the motley crowd tumbled into the room.

Mr Melamed recognized the Bow Street Runner, who was hauling behind him the Earl of Gravel Lane. He recognized, as well, Lady Marblehead and Mr Clyde. The short, balding man he was unfamiliar with, but a mouthed hint from General Well'ngone informed him that the person was Mr Waters.

Saulty had sprung up from the sofa, ostensibly to give way to his betters but actually to try and sneak away before his presence was noticed. A withering look from the Earl made him stay in the room.

The General did not bother to sneak away. At the present moment he was at the centre of the group's attention, since Mr Waters was pointing at him and shouting, "There he is! There he is! That is the boy I saw sneaking about my rooms! Ask him where the papers are!"

"Well, boy, where is it?" Lady Marblehead chimed in. "What have you done with my will?"

The General, who had learned well from the Earl of Gravel Lane how to greet even the direst situation with aplomb, was not at all bothered by the hue and cry. "I beg your pardon, madam," he icily replied. "Have we been introduced?"

"This isn't a dance at Almack's," growled the Bow Street Runner. "Answer Lady Marblehead's question."

The Bow Street Runner might have said more, had not Mr Clyde stepped into the centre of the fray and said, "Aunt, this is not good manners. We have barged into Mr Melamed's home without offering a word of explanation for our presence. Allow me to explain to our host why we have come, before this officer of the law throttles the child."

"There is no need to explain," snorted Mr Waters. "If the boy is here, it is obvious that this man is also involved in the plot."

"Why should Mr Melamed wish to steal my aunt's will?" asked Mr Clyde.

"Why should anyone wish to steal Lady Marblehead's will?" asked the Earl of Gravel Lane, shaking his arm free from the Bow Street Runner's grip. "Can it be pawned? Can it be sold on the open market, traded for fruitcakes, perhaps? This entertainment verges upon the ridiculous. If it were performed upon the stage, we should all be pelted by rotten tomatoes."

While the Earl brushed away some imaginary vegetables from his threadbare sleeve, Mr Melamed said, "Perhaps, Mr Clyde, if you would be good enough to explain why you are all here."

"It would be my pleasure, sir. Last night, my aunt surprised me with an offer to increase what I might expect to inherit when she has gone to that better world. This morning, seeing that the weather was fine, I suggested we not postpone the visit to her solicitor to arrange for a new will. She agreed, we went, but to our surprise, when Mr Waters went to retrieve the box with the Marblehead papers he discovered, to his shock, that the box was missing."

"No!" exclaimed General Well'ngone. "Missing?"

"May I assume that you all went to Bow Street to report the loss?" asked Mr Melamed.

"You may, sir," said Mr Clyde.

"And whose idea was it that the Earl of Gravel Lane was responsible for the theft?"

"Mine, sir," said Mr Waters.

"Why?"

"I told you, sir. I saw that good-for-nothing bicorne-hatted companion of his hanging about my door. What was the boy doing there, if he was not up to trouble?"

"But what interest could the Earl have had in Lady Marblehead's will? As the Earl mentioned just a minute ago, a will is not something that can be sold or pawned."

"My theory, Mr Melamed, is that the Earl and his gang were working for you. It is a well-known fact that you are a friend of Mr Powell, and I happen to know that Mr Powell would be very happy, indeed, to get his hands on that will."

"That is possibly true," said Mr Melamed. He then turned to Lady Marblehead and said, "So it is really Mr Powell that you are accusing of this theft. Would it not better serve your purpose if this officer of the law went to Mr Powell's home and arrested your cousin?"

At the mention of Mr Powell's name and the family connection, Lady Marblehead turned purple. "No, it would not, Mr Melamed." She then turned to her great-nephew and said, "Clyde, call the carriage. We are going home at once. And as for you, sir, Mr Waters, find that will by tomorrow or I shall have you thrown in gaol for carelessness."

Lady Marblehead, followed by Mr Clyde, flounced out of the room. Mr Waters looked as though he wished to say something, but upon seeing that the Bow Street Runner was still in the room he decided against it and left, as well.

"Is there anything else I can do for you?" Mr Melamed asked the officer.

The Bow Street Runner glared at the Earl of Gravel Lane and said, "One day, Earl, one day I'll catch you." And then he stormed out of the room.

The tension in the room was lowered considerably after the departure of those guests, but Mr Melamed was far from feeling at ease. "I did not ask you to steal the will," he said to the Earl. "Why did you not bring it to me last night to read, and then return it?"

"Mr Waters had made a prior request for us to steal it."

"Why on earth would he do that?"

"He didn't say," said the Earl, spicing his words with a shrug that seemed to say, "I am above the frivolous cares and caprices of the world."

"I assume that you did find out what the will said."

"Naturally. Mr Powell's son inherits the bulk of Lady Marblehead's property."

"And Mr Clyde?"

"A mere trifle."

The Earl waited a moment for Mr Melamed to digest this piece of information, before saying, "It was our theory, last night, that Mr Clyde preferred that the will never be found. Since he is the closest blood relative, he would then inherit everything. But that was last night."

~ 169 ~

"Yes, if that was the plot, he wouldn't have wanted Lady Marblehead to make a new will. Mostly likely the woman would not have disinherited Thomas Powell entirely, so the most that Mr Clyde could have hoped for, in that instance, was to equally share the wealth. No, there must be another reason for Mr Waters's behaviour. Where is the will now?"

"It is in a box, with some other papers."

"And where is the box? Perhaps the other papers will shed some light on the matter."

"We gave the box to Jeremiah, the old clothes man, to hide."

"Find him at once and bring him here, with the box."

General Well'ngone, who had been quiet until then, stepped forward and said, "Mr Melamed, there is something else that happened last night."

"Well?"

"Mr Taylor is a madman!" Saulty blurted out. "A maniac! A murderer!"

"Not so loud, Saulty," said the General. "We haven't pawned our ears."

"What is he talking about?"

"It's like this, Mr Melamed," said General Well'ngone, "after we paid a visit to the rooms of Mr Waters, we decided to go to Bury Street to pay a visit to the rooms of Mr Taylor."

"I saw you. The window over there overlooks the alley," he said, pointing to the back wall of the library.

"Then maybe you saw Jeremiah, the old clothes man, leave Mr Taylor's room with a bundle in his hand."

"I did. What of it?"

"It's what was in it that's important."

"Very well, what was in it?"

"A dead body!" screamed Saulty.

Mr Melamed stared at the boy, wondering if the child was merely frightened or totally insane.

"Don't think of carting him off to the asylum, Mr Melamed. He's not insane," said the General. "We both heard someone screaming inside the room. Then I saw the knife in Mr Taylor's hand. And then all was silent. Afterward, old Jeremiah came out with a bundle - we all saw it, even you, Mr Melamed - and we followed, Saulty and I, we followed him in the dead of night all the way to the old Jewish cemetery on Alderney Road, where he took a spade and dug a hole and buried that poor bundle in a dark, damp, deserted, and definitely unmarked Jewish grave."

For several long moments Mr Melamed was speechless. "You saw him do it?"

"I saw it with these two peepers, as clear as I'm now seeing you."

Mr Melamed collapsed into a chair. His face was deathly pale. "I cannot believe it. There must be some misunderstanding."

"You forgot to mention something, General Well'ngone," said the Earl, who made a gesture of encircling his wrist with his other hand.

"You found the bracelet?" asked Mr Melamed, without enthusiasm. "Where?"

"It was in a cabinet in that room that Mr Taylor uses for his murderous experiments on innocent young children," said General Well'ngone.

"Where is the bracelet now?"

"He gave it to Jeremiah."

"You didn't search Jeremiah's rooms?"

"We did, but the bracelet wasn't there," said the Earl. "I would have sent for Jeremiah this morning, to ask about the bracelet - perhaps he buried it with the papers - if I hadn't had the unexpected pleasure of receiving Lady Marblehead and her company."

"Find him," said Mr Melamed. "And find Mr Taylor."

* * *

After the initial shock of the morning had worn off, Mr Melamed set to work. He knew he must pay a visit to the Jewish cemetery and find what had been buried there the previous night, but it was necessary to do so without making the visit too public. The head of the *Chevrah Kaddisha*, the Jewish Burial Society, must be informed. He also wished for there to be two other witnesses when the grave was opened. He therefore composed letters to Mr Lyon and Mr Baer, begging their pardons for asking them to leave their places of work, while assuring them that the request was not a trivial one. He had just finished sealing the letters, when his butler entered and said that a Mr Accum wished to see him.

"Show him in, and arrange for these letters to be hand-delivered immediately."

In truth, Mr Melamed was not certain he would be able to concentrate on what Mr Accum had to say, since his mind was flying in a thousand directions. But Mr Accum, although a man of science, was apparently oblivious to the electrified atmosphere in the room; he sat down with calm assurance, removed a paper from his coat pocket with calm assurance, and proceeded to read his notes with that same calm assurance, seemingly certain that Mr Melamed could have no other interest than to hear Mr Accum's report.

"The pickles were just as I thought," he said with satisfaction. "They were full of a copper substance; verdigris, perhaps you have heard of it. No? Well, it is a pity the public is not better informed. But that is a topic for another day. On this day, I have written to Mr and Mrs Franks and advised them to throw out the pickles at once. I have found copper in the green-coloured candies, as well. Stay away from foods that are brightly-coloured green, Mr Melamed, if you value your stomach and your health."

"Yes, but Lady Marblehead does not eat pickles. And we have no proof that she ate candies from this confectionary. Did you find anything wrong with the foods in her pantry?"

"No," said the man of science with a shrug. "Her illness remains a mystery. Shall I visit the kitchen of the Jewish orphanage?"

"Yes, I will write you a letter of introduction. The cook's name is Mrs Halberstein. She may still be upset that she was accused of poisoning the children by serving them some tainted fish, so please try not to offend her any further."

"I could visit the kitchen after she has gone home for the night."

"No. I would like your report by this evening, if that is not asking too much."

"I am at your service, sir. Perhaps you wish to subscribe to a pamphlet I write concerning my scientific work?"

Mr Melamed wrote the man of science a generous check.

CHAPTER XVI

When Mr Melamed's letter arrived at the clock-making establishment owned by Mr Lyon, the proprietor was engaged in a conversation with three important visitors, one of whom was crying louder than all the chimes in England, or so it seemed.

"Take Isaac to the back room, Hannah," said Mr Lyon. "The child will not stop crying until he has had some nourishment."

While Hannah went to feed the baby, the other visitor, Miss Rebecca Lyon—for the two sisters had gone out for a drive, since it was a beautiful spring day—amused herself by observing the mechanical show being put on by one of the mantelpiece clocks. She was not so enthralled, though, by the performance that her eyes did not follow the footsteps of the messenger who entered the shop and delivered a letter into her father's hands. A letter is always a matter of interest.

Miss Lyon observed her father's face, and saw a mild expression of annoyance mar his usually genial looks.

"Mr Warburg?" he called out. A young man who was his assistant appeared at the door that led to the workshop where small repairs were made. "I am afraid I must leave the shop in your hands today, as well."

"Yes, sir," said Mr Warburg.

"Lord Dangerfield is sending round a messenger for his library clock this afternoon. Please make sure the parcel is ready." Mr Lyon then added, "I may not return before closing time, but you know what to do."

Mr Warburg gave a slight bow and then returned to his duties.

"Have you and Hannah finished with your shopping?" Mr Lyon asked Rebecca. "I must go to Bury Street. We could travel together if you are ready to return home."

Rebecca, sensing that something important was brewing, thought she would very much prefer to go to Bury Street than to visit more shops. But when Hannah returned and showed disappointment at the idea, since she very much wanted to buy a ribbon for a cap she was making for Isaac and someone must hold the baby while she was inspecting all the wares that would be on display in the shop, Rebecca was forced to put aside her own desire and defer to the needs of the child, for how could he be seen in public wearing a ribbon-less cap?

It is an awesome responsibility to be an aunt.

* * *

Mr Baer was already sitting in Mr Melamed's library when Mr Lyon arrived. Mr Melamed began the distasteful meeting by first thanking the two men for their quick response to his summons.

"I should not have done it, if …" He was at a momentary loss for words. Then he looked at the two waiting faces—they were men he had known for years — and decided that the best way was to hide nothing. "There is a suspicion that Mr Taylor has been conducting medical experiments on street children."

Mr Lyon and Mr Baer were too shocked to respond.

"I have been informed that a child may have been killed and buried in the Alderney Cemetery last night. I intend to go to the cemetery now, where Mr Hirsch, who is a member of the *Chevrah Kaddisha* will be waiting for me. I would like there to be witnesses when the grave is opened, which is why I summoned you. Will you go with me?"

The two men gave their grim consent. Mr Melamed's carriage, which was waiting for them, conveyed them down Whitechapel Street. Inside that carriage, the three men were as silent as if they had been riding inside a hearse, G-d forbid. When they reached the cemetery, Mr Hirsch was waiting for them at the gate, which stood open.

The little group, still shrouded in silence, made their way to the far wall. The two gravediggers, standing at the spot where the earth had been opened the night before, showed the others the way to their destination.

"It is easy to spot a freshly dug grave," Mr Hirsch explained, when they had arrived. "Shall I tell the men to begin?"

Mr Melamed gave his assent. They two gravediggers were experienced at their work, and it did not take them long to find the bundle. Yet when the swaddled object came into view, the thought crossed more than one mind that they would rather not see what was inside. But they had given their word to witness the unwrapping, and could not turn away at this important moment.

One of the gravediggers saw their hesitation and took command of the situation. He bent down and took hold of the linen cloth. It took him only a minute to unwind what had been hastily wound the night before. When he got his first look at what was hidden inside, he gave a whistle.

"What is it?" asked Mr Melamed. "We must see, as well."

The gravedigger lifted the box from its hastily dug grave and handed it to Mr Melamed.

"Would you take off the lid, Mr Baer?"

Mr Baer did so, and the entire group gave a sigh of relief, since there was nothing gruesome about the sight that greeted their eyes. Indeed, Mr Melamed looked upon the contents with great interest.

"We shall examine this more closely at my home," he said to his relieved witnesses. He then thanked Mr Hirsch for his trouble and paid the gravediggers for their work.

"I suppose you did not see the person who dug this grave," said Mr Melamed, after he had handed the men the coins.

"No, sir," said the first gravedigger. "It was dug after we left. But there was something a bit odd that happened earlier in the day."

"What was that?"

"We found Mr Taylor wandering around."

"Wandering?"

"Not exactly wandering, sir," said the second gravedigger. "He was sitting on that bench over there."

"And you thought that odd?"

~ 177 ~

"Well, what was he doing there, sitting all by himself? It's not as if he has family buried here, and so he came to pay his respects. And he wasn't sitting near the grave of Rabbi Falk or Rabbi Schiff, the way people sometimes do come when they want to make a request and say a little prayer. So what was he doing here?"

The gravedigger gave Mr Melamed a knowing look. "I wouldn't be surprised if those papers had something to do with that poison business. Evidence, I believe they call it."

Mr Melamed said nothing. He merely walked away, and the others followed. They were already near the front gate, when they heard a cry from behind them. One of the gravediggers was waving the white sheet that had swaddled the box, while the second one was running toward them.

"Mr Melamed!" the second man called. "Look at this!"

Mr Melamed turned to see what the man was holding in his hand. It was a pearl bracelet.

* * *

Both Mr Melamed and Mr Lyon were men of business who had had their share of experiences with the Exchange and investing in business ventures, some of which involved speculations in distant lands. While Mr Melamed had generally done well with his investments, Mr Lyon could not say the same. An unwise investment in South America had nearly sent him and his family to debtors' prison. He therefore observed the papery story unfolding before their eyes with a mixture of fascination and horror.

"I still do not understand how he did it, or why," said Mr Baer, who tended his coffee house and made do with the proceeds from that kosher establishment. Somehow there was always enough, thanks to the kindness of Hashem, even though there seemed to be a new arrival to the Baer household every other year.

Mr Melamed pointed to the multitude of business documents that were at that moment covering his desk. "The will is clear," said Mr Melamed, taking up that document. "Thomas Powell inherits the bulk of the Marblehead fortune, including both the property and the monies invested in securities and other speculations. Mr Clyde receives a small inheritance, to be taken from some of the investments. The theft is also clear. Over the years, Mr Waters, the family's solicitor, abused the family's trust. He forged the signatures of both Lord and Lady Marblehead to sell shares, without their knowledge, and used the money to invest in the Exchange himself."

"And none too successfully," Mr Lyon added.

"In plains words, Mr Waters has lost all of Lady Marblehead's money?" asked Mr Baer.

"I could not have stated it better," said Mr Melamed.

"Then neither Thomas Powell nor Mr Clyde will inherit a thing, when Lady Marblehead dies."

"They will not inherit any money, Mr Baer, but there is still the property and the contents of the house in Mayfair. Unless there are significant debts to pay, Thomas Powell will inherit that."

Mr Baer digested this information in silence for several minutes. Then he asked, "Do you think Mr Clyde knew about what Waters had done?"

~ 179 ~

"I should not think so. I believe he was sincere in his efforts to have a new will written, one which would be in his favour."

"He will be one disappointed young man when the truth is discovered."

"So will Thomas Powell," said Mr Lyon.

Mr Melamed silently agreed. He had not told his friends about the gambling debt that was hanging over the young man's head. The loss of the Marblehead fortune would be a blow.

"But at least he will inherit something," Mr Lyon added, holding the pearl bracelet up to catch the light. "If this bracelet has companions of a similar quality, Mr Thomas Powell will have quite a nice treasure chest to present to his bride."

"Is there a connection between the bracelet and the papers, other than the fact that Jeremiah buried them both?" asked Mr Baer.

"I do not yet know," replied Mr Melamed. "But our work today has not been wasted. At least we do know that Mr Taylor is not murdering children in his laboratory."

"Will you tell Mr Powell?" asked Mr Lyon. "It might be better if he confronts Waters and not you. After all, it is his fortune that was stolen."

"True, but there is a problem: the box was stolen by General Well'ngone and two of the Earl's boys. Even though it was at the instigation of Mr Waters, I cannot be sure that the law will treat the General and the others with compassion."

"So what will you do?"

"At the moment, I shall do nothing. Mr Waters's theft of the Marblehead fortune must be dealt with, but we have more pressing matters. We still do not know what is causing this illness. If Mr Clyde and Mr Taylor have been working in concert to poison Lady Marblehead, even if Clyde inherits nothing it is still a crime."

"You therefore think the bracelet was a payment to Mr Taylor?"

"I think it is time that I must have a talk with Mr Taylor. He must be somewhere. He cannot elude me forever."

Mr Melamed was escorting his guests to the door, when that door was assaulted from the outside by a loud and persistent knocking. That knocking was accompanied by the sounds of a child screaming, "Open up! Open the door!"

Mr Melamed opened the door himself, and Simon nearly tumbled to the ground, at his feet. But the child quickly recovered his balance, if not his composure.

"He's dying, Mr Melamed, he's dying! Why don't you do anything? Why won't anybody help him?"

"Who is dying, Simon?"

"Ezekiel," said the child, and then he broke down into tears.

"We're going to the orphanage now." Mr Melamed then turned to Mr Lyon and said, "Another physician must see the child. Can you go to Mr Obadiah and persuade him to come to the orphanage immediately?"

"He is no longer seeing patients, but perhaps this once he will."

While Mr Lyon went off in search of the elderly physician, whose retirement from service had led to the employment of Mr Taylor, the others went out to the street, where Mr Melamed's carriage was waiting.

But yet another obstacle presented itself before they could set off, this time in the form of Mr Clyde.

"Mr Melamed, one minute, sir, of your time, if I may," said the young man.

"I am very busy at the moment, Mr Clyde. Can your business wait?"

"It is about the pearl bracelet. I believe I know where it is."

"I shall call upon you later."

"But the bracelet is not in Mayfair. If my informant is correct, the bracelet is here, on Bury Street."

"Then you may call upon me later, sir." Mr Melamed climbed into the carriage and shut the door. "The orphanage," he called out to his coachman, "and hurry!"

CHAPTER XVII

When Mr Melamed's carriage pulled up in front of the orphanage, Mr Muller was surprised to see Simon climb down from it. But before he could scold the child, Mr Melamed asked, "Is Mr Taylor here? I wish to see him."

"He finally turned up this morning, Mr Melamed. He is presently with Ezekiel. The child is very ill."

Mr Melamed turned to Simon and said, "Go down to the kitchen. Tell Mrs Halberstein to give you something to eat. If she asks by whose orders, say the request comes from me."

Simon did not move.

"If you wish to help your friend, fly!"

Simon flew.

"Mr Baer, wait here for Mr Obadiah." Mr Melamed then explained to Mr Muller, as the two men walked down the hall, he wished a second physician to examine the child.

"I should have liked to call in Mr Obadiah earlier," said Mr Muller as he hopped down the hall, trying to keep up with Mr Melamed's longer strides. "But the expense, dear me, it is hard enough to manage with one physician, let alone two, and I ..."

They had reached the door to the sick room, and Mr Melamed signalled to Mr Muller to be quiet. Mr Taylor, who had been sitting at Ezekiel's bedside, staring vacantly down at the child's pinched and grey face, looked up at the sound of their voices.

"Mr Taylor, I would like to have a word with you, if you can leave the child for a few minutes."

Even in the dim light of the sickroom, Mr Melamed could see that the physician seemed to have aged several years since he had last seen the young man.

"I am not much use to the child anyway," said Mr Taylor as he rose from his seat.

Mr Melamed did not respond to that, but he did ask Mr Muller to take Mr Taylor's place by the sick child, and the orphanage director reluctantly obeyed.

"I have asked Mr Obadiah to come and take a look at the child," said Mr Melamed, as he and Mr Taylor walked back toward the entrance of the orphanage.

"I hope he shall be able to save Ezekiel." Mr Taylor's voice was as dull as his eyes. It was as if all the life inside him was seeping out, along with the life of the deathly ill child.

"Mr Taylor, I must you some questions. They are painful for me to ask. They will be painful for you to hear and to answer. But it must be done."

"I am at your service, sir."

"We will start with the pearl bracelet. How did it come to be in your laboratory?"

"How did you know?" the young man blurted out, clearly startled that Mr Melamed was aware of this information.

"Never mind how I know. How did it get there?"

"I do not know."

"Do not try to deceive me, Mr Taylor. I know more about this business than you think."

"Then you know more than I do, Mr Melamed. I never saw that bracelet before last night. I have no idea who it belongs to, no idea why someone put it my cabinet, and no idea why you are interested in it. Does my answer satisfy you?"

It did not, but Mr Melamed was happy to see that a bit of colour had returned to the young man's cheeks and a bit of life to his sunken spirits.

"Would you have me believe then that you were not acquainted with Mr Clyde in Jamaica?"

Mr Taylor stopped and stared a second time. "How on earth …"

The young man could not finish his sentence for at that moment the door to the orphanage was flung open and Mr Waters stormed into the hall.

"I want a word with you, Mr Melamed," said the solicitor.

"If you will wait in the sitting room, Mr Waters, I will join you there after I have finished speaking to Mr Taylor."

"What I have to say concerns the both of you," snarled the solicitor, although he was careful to keep that snarl to a muffled whisper. "You and I both know, Mr Melamed, who stole the box with Lady Marblehead's will. By now you probably know what else was inside that box, besides the will. I therefore have a business proposition to make to you. Make good the money that I have lost, so that no one need ever know what I have done, and I will not prosecute your little friend with the bicorne hat. Neither will I tell the magistrate that this person you have employed is nothing more than a lying, scheming quack doctor!"

"Liar!" shouted Mr Taylor. "How dare you?"

While Mr Melamed tried to stop the physician from attacking the solicitor, a small crowd had begun to assemble in the front hallway. Miss Taylor, who had heard her brother scream, had run to see what had happened; at the same moment, Mr Obadiah and Mr Lyon, who had spotted old Jeremiah on a street and grabbed him, had just arrived and they paused at the doorway to stare. Following them was Mr Clyde, who had arrived at the orphanage on foot.

Meanwhile, Mr Waters, abandoning his attempt at secrecy, shouted at the top of his lungs, "I know who you are, and that sister of yours, too! From Jamaica, my eye! A doctor, my foot! You were spawned in the gutters of London, and got your education in its streets. You're the children of that old clothes man standing over there! He rents rooms in one of the buildings I own near Gravel Lane. I have seen the two of you there, sneaking in and out, trying to avoid paying the extra rent. Is not what I say the truth, Jeremiah Schneider? Am I not your landlord? Do you not rent from me a room?"

"That much of your long speech is true, Mr Waters," said Jeremiah. "I do have the pleasure of resting my weary bones in that rat-infested, dirt-encrusted hovel that you own but do not deign to improve. But to say that Mr Taylor and Miss Taylor are my children, why it makes a person laugh! Maybe Mr Taylor had pity on me once or twice and brought me an ointment or a draught for the fever. And maybe Miss Taylor, the kind soul that she is, brought me a drop of soup. But to infer from those charitable visits that these two young people are related to someone like me — why anyone can see that they have been raised in genteel society, that their parents must have been well-educated and refined people, while I am no one, nothing, only an old and weary old clothes man."

"That is not so, grandfather."

All eyes turned to Mr Taylor.

"No, Mr Taylor, don't …" Jeremiah protested.

"The masquerade is over, sir. Mr Schneider is my grandfather, Mr Melamed, and I am proud to be his grandson. I am only sorry that he would not let me and my sister acknowledge the relationship before this. He was under the mistaken apprehension that if word got out that my father's father was an old clothes man, it would hinder my career. But since I seem to have ruined that career of my own accord, there is no longer a reason to not admit the relationship."

Mr Melamed noted that Miss Taylor had gone over to Jeremiah, who was looking as if he might start to cry. He then said to Mr Taylor, "Is it then true that you did not grow up in Jamaica, and that you did not attend medical school?"

"On the contrary, Miss Taylor and I did grow up there. My parents moved to Jamaica after they married, hoping to improve their position in life. They were only moderately successful. My father did not have the temperament to be a plantation owner. And so when he and our mother both died of the fever in the same year, there was not much of an inheritance. My sister graciously agreed that I could use the little money we had to train as a physician. That part of the story is also true."

"Is there anyone who can vouch for your word, Mr Taylor? Is there anyone in London who knew you and Miss Taylor when you were living in Jamaica?"

Mr Clyde stepped forward. "I can."

The moment that Mr Melamed had dreaded almost from the first had finally arrived. As he had suspected, there was a connection between the two young men, and he inwardly shuddered to think what it might be. The bracelet found in the cemetery, the way Mr Taylor's face had turned deathly pale when Mr Clyde stepped forward, warned him to expect the worst. But before he could ask the next and obvious question, Mr Accum, dragging Mrs Halberstein behind him, ran into the hall, waving a flask in his other hand.

"I have found it! Mr Melamed, I have found it," the man of science happily exclaimed, totally oblivious to the sombre faces that surrounded him. "It was the copper! I knew it! The mystery is solved!"

Mr Melamed, irritated by this distraction, hurriedly said, "I am very happy for you, Mr Accum. You have my congratulations on your scientific discovery, but right now I am trying to determine who it is that is poisoning these children."

"That is what I am trying to tell you, sir, I have found the culprit."

"What?" asked a dazed Mr Melamed, who seemed to see Mrs Halberstein for the first time. "Surely not ..."

"It wasn't me, sir," the poor lady wailed. "I didn't intend to do it. How could I know? How could I know?"

"Know what? Would one of you explain, please?"

"That is what I am trying to do," said Mr Accum. "The answer is right here in this flask. I told you to be suspicious of any food that is too green. It is like the snake. On the outside it shimmers in the light, but inside — bah!"

Somewhere within the inner chambers of Mr Melamed's mind a memory stirred. The Rebbe, in his letter, had mentioned a snake. But where was it? Where?

"Where?" he heard himself saying. "This snake, where is it?"

"There!" said Mr Accum, pointing to a tin that Mrs Halberstein was holding.

"I didn't know, sir," the woman continued to sob, as Mr Melamed approached her. "It was Mr Muller, sir. He was the one who said to use it. It was much cheaper than the other ones, he said. And we got some as a gift, so we had plenty on hand. I thought it would be a treat for the children, seeing how they were so sick. I didn't mean to harm the poor lambs. I didn't mean to …"

Her voice, and all the other sounds in the world, seemed to fade away as Mr Melamed's eyes focused on the tin that the woman was holding in her hand. He took the tin, barely noticing the gay and colourful writing on it, and opened the lid. He shook some of the tin's contents into the palm of his hand. For a moment he thought he must be going mad, for he saw a dozen or more tiny snakes writhing against his skin.

"Look at the colour, Mr Melamed," Mr Accum was whispering in his ear. "When the good Lord made tea leaves, He never made any that are that colour green."

"It is these leaves that have been making the children so ill? It was tea?"

"The children haven't been drinking tea, sir. They've been drinking poison."

The silence that followed was only broken when Mr Muller came into the foyer. "Mr Taylor, someone, Ezekiel is crying. Mrs Halberstein, what are you doing standing here? The child is calling for something to drink. Bring him a cup of tea."

Mr Muller was never quite sure what it was that he had said to cause such a reaction. Whenever he told this story, and in the ensuing years he told it many times, he would explain, without being able to explain why, that the halls of the orphanage suddenly resounded with the piercing cry of a half dozen or more people shouting as one, "NO!"

CHAPTER XVIII

While Mr Taylor and Mr Obadiah tended to Ezekiel, Mr Melamed and Mr Lyon went off to collect samples of tea leaves from the pantries of the Franks and Marblehead residences. Mr Baer was sent to check the pantry of the tea room where the members of the Jewish Ladies' Charitable Auxiliary had held their meeting. The samples were brought to Mr Accum's laboratory, where he showed the gentlemen how he had discovered that the tea leaves had been tampered with. He explained that there were unscrupulous people who collected tea leaves that had already been used from the cooks who worked in coffee houses and hotels, who sold the used leaves for a small price. Those leaves were then boiled with copperas and sheep's dung. Afterward, a dye was added to give the leaves a more appealing colour, such as verdigris, a copper acetate that turns leaves green. Sometime tea leaves were not used at all, and other dried leaves were boiled and dyed to make the so-called tea.

Reader, I wish I could explain to you in greater detail the interesting experiment that Mr Accum did in his laboratory, which conclusively showed that some of the samples of tea leaves had been too highly saturated with containments. Mr Lyon tried to replicate the experiment in his home in Devonshire

Square, before the adoring eyes of his wife and children. Unfortunately, the flask exploded and the tablecloth caught on fire before the experiment was concluded, and Mrs Lyon said, in a voice that brooked no argument, that this was the last time that a scientific experiment would be attempted in *her* home.

I therefore advise you to turn to Mr Accum's most interesting pamphlet on the subject, if you would like more information. You may contact him though Mr Ackermann's Repository for the Arts, 101 Strand, London, England, to request a copy.

To resume our narrative, for that is our real business, let us assume that the experiment in Mr Accum's laboratory has been concluded, and Mr Lyon and Mr Baer have departed. However, Mr Melamed has remained, since he has a few more questions to ask the man of science.

"Mr Accum, I still do not understand. If your assumption is that there are many unscrupulous merchants who are selling adulterated tea leaves, why is not all London sick to death?"

"It is a question of degree, Mr Melamed. A small amount of verdigris will cause a small amount of discomfort if the tea is drunk in moderation, or it could cause none at all if a person has a strong constitution. But if the manufacturer making the mixture gets the amount wrong, as this tea merchant apparently did, at least in some of his tins, it can be a disaster for people who are more delicate, as you have seen."

Mr Melamed stared down at the tins that had been collected from the orphanage, the tea room, the

Franks home, and Lady Marblehead's residence. The tins of tea had all come from the same place.

"Thank you, Mr Accum, you have done the Jewish community of London a great service," said Mr Melamed as he rose to go.

"I only hope the little boy can be saved."

"I do, too."

* * *

Mr Melamed did not return to the orphanage immediately. Instead, he instructed his coachman to take him to the address that was written on the tin of tea. When the tumbledown warren of streets became too narrow for a carriage to pass through, he instructed the coachman to wait while he went the rest of the way on foot. Inside one of the dingy courtyards, he found the place that he was looking for: Amos & Amos, Tea Merchants.

Mr Lazer Amos and Mr Baruch Amos were eating their supper when Mr Melamed entered their place of work. Through an open doorway, Mr Melamed could also see into what appeared to be the factory's workroom. There, a small boy who looked to be no more than seven or eight years old was stirring a large pot, which was presumably filled with spent tea leaves that would soon receive a second life. The sight of the boy, who unknowingly held the fate of countless lives in his small hands, made Mr Melamed feel quite sick with the utter irresponsibility of it all; a single false movement, adding too much of the verdigris, for example, could turn the company's tea leaves into a dangerous poison, and no one would know it.

~ 193 ~

Mr Lazer Amos did not recognize their visitor, but Mr Baruch Amos did and he immediately stood up and went to the door.

"Mr Melamed, this is an honour," said the tea merchant, "but what did I tell you, eh? Amos & Amos, remember the name, sir, for one day you will be calling on me and not I on you. Now that day has come, I see, and it is my pleasure, sir, my honour, sir, to ask you, sir, what may I do for you, sir? You have not come for one tin of tea, not a busy man like you. Is it a dozen tins you need, two dozen … three?"

By this time even an ebullient soul such as Mr Baruch Amos had realized that something was amiss. As his voice trailed away, his brother said, "Shut your mouth, Baruch. Let the gentleman speak."

"Mr Amos, I understand you are the brains behind this venture," Mr Melamed said to the man named Lazer. "If that is so, I have come to make you an offer. I would like to buy your business. I am willing to offer you ten pounds."

The two brothers exchanged glances. Mr Baruch Amos, regaining some of his ebullience, said, "But Mr Melamed, you must be joking. Ten pounds for a thriving enterprise like this? Why only yesterday a gentleman came here and stood on the very spot where you are standing now and …"

"Shut up, Baruch," said Mr Lazer Amos, who was examining Mr Melamed with a hard eye. "Why do you wish to buy my business, sir?"

"Because your tea is contaminated, Mr Amos; it is only thanks to Hashem's mercy that you have not yet committed murder. I wish to close you down before you add that crime to whatever other sins you have committed."

Mr Baruch Amos was about to protest, when a look from his brother made him close his mouth and let Lazer speak.

"Some people might say that is a libellous claim, Mr Melamed. I hope you have proof to back up your words."

"I do. I have proof that your tea almost killed a peeress of the realm."

"Almost?" said Mr Baruch Amos with a nervous laugh and a shrug. "People *almost* die every day. Why, I was nearly run over by a carriage just the day before last, and I ..."

Mr Melamed grabbed the too-talkative tea merchant by the coat and shook him. "Do you not understand? You have poisoned a child with that tea of yours! Either except my offer of ten pounds now, and burn that filth of yours that you call tea leaves, and give me your word that you will never sell the stuff again—or, if that child dies, I shall drag the two of you to Bow Street and turn you over to the magistrate, who will, no doubt, be pleased to turn you over to the hangman."

"He's bluffing, Lazer, isn't he? Our tea is the finest tea in the world, for the price that is. Isn't that what you told me to say, Lazer? It's a fine product, isn't that right? Lazer?"

Mr Melamed, not waiting for the other brother to respond, took the merchant by the sleeve and pulled him through the alleyway and into his carriage. Fortunately, his mind was too concerned with other matters to hear the nervous chatter of the tea merchant, who alternated between bravado and faint-heartedness in the most alarming manner.

The tea merchant was in his bravado mode when the carriage drove up to the orphanage's door. Perhaps he could not believe that a wealthy man like Mr Melamed would truly care about the woes of one small orphan, but whatever the reason, he had been restored to his former self as he strode with Mr Melamed down to the corridor.

When they reached the room where Ezekiel slept, Mr Melamed motioned for the two physicians to stand to the side so that Mr Baruch Amos could have a clear view of the child.

"Ezekiel," said Mr Melamed, "you have a visitor."

"Now then, my boy," said Mr Amos, pulling a chair up to the bedside and sitting upon it, "what's all this? I have boys myself, little Ezekiel, so you can't fool me. They like to sleep late on a spring morning, too. Pretend they're too ill to help with the work, but the minute my back is turned they've snuck off to have their bit of pleasure in the big, wide world. I know a slacker when I see one, Ezekiel, my boy, so you stop this nonsense and get out of bed. If you don't do as I say, I'll take that little hand of yours and drag you ..."

Mr Amos did as he said and took Ezekiel's hand. The coldness made the merchant drop it in an instant. "Well, Ezekiel, my boy, maybe I spoke too soon," said Mr Amos, small beads of perspiration appearing on his forehead, "maybe you aren't feeling as right as you should be. But come on, lad, pluck up your spirits. It can't be as bad as all that. Tell the gentlemen here you've been shamming just a wee bit. ... They'll understand. ... We were all young once. We ..."

The serious of the situation had finally made itself clear. Mr Amos raised his eyes and howled, "*Mein*

Gott in Himmel! I didn't mean any harm! Dear G-d, don't let this child die. Don't let him die."

* * *

Mr Melamed had not forgotten his promise to call upon Mr Clyde, but first he paid a visit to his friend, Mr Powell.

"I shall leave it to you and Lady Marblehead to decide what to do about Mr Waters," he said, after he had shown Mr Powell the papers and given over the box.

"I suppose she must be told, although it will be a shock," said Mr Powell, who was looking rather shocked himself.

Lady Marblehead heard the news with a stoicism that surprised the two gentlemen. "Then I truly am poor?" she asked quietly.

"I am afraid so, ma'am," said Mr Powell. "But the house is yours, as are your jewels and the silver and everything else that is in it."

Lady Marblehead laughed. "Not everything in it, Powell. When Mr Clyde hears the news, I am sure he will forget that he was ever a relation of mine."

Indeed, Mr Clyde at first refused to believe that Mr Powell was telling him the truth. But at last he was forced to admit that the papers were genuine, and his amiable disposition seemed to vanish along with his hopes of securing a fortune.

Mr Melamed had no desire to remain in that unhappy house a moment longer than he had to, but there was still one matter which had to be cleared up. "Mr Clyde, you hinted that you knew the pearl bracelet was in Mr Taylor's laboratory. Perhaps you will explain how you knew that information."

"I knew because I hired a child to put it there. I had heard that Mr Taylor sometimes tended to street urchins without payment, and so I told this child to pretend to be ill. He slipped it into a cabinet when Mr Taylor was not looking."

"May I ask why you did this?"

"You asked, earlier today, if there was anyone who could vouch that Mr and Miss Taylor had lived in Jamaica. If you will recall, I said that I could. I had the pleasure of making the acquaintance of Miss Taylor a few months before she and her brother left for Europe. I fell in love with the lady and asked her brother for her hand. He refused me, saying that the young lady would never marry out of her faith. At the time I did not believe him. I knew he intended to study medicine in Europe, and that he expected Miss Taylor to run his household for him. I therefore thought he had refused my offer of marriage out of selfishness—he did not want me to interfere with his plans.

"I have since spoken to Miss Taylor—I met her one day at Lady Marblehead's home, when she came to deliver a draught for my great-aunt, in place of her brother - and from her own lips I learned that what her brother had said was true, she had no wish to marry me. I am not a man who accepts an insult to my honour lightly. I therefore decided to take my revenge upon them both. While Lady Marblehead was ill, I had many opportunities to remove the bracelet; it was nothing, really, a child could have done it without being caught. I thought it would be just as easy to ensure that the blame fell upon Mr

Taylor. I should have enjoyed seeing him on the gallows, whether it was for the supposed theft, the supposed poisoning of my dear aunt, or both. But I did not take into account your interest in the matter, Mr Melamed."

"You would have sent an innocent man to the gallows?" asked Mr Powell, who despite his dislike for the young man had not suspected him capable of such contemptible behaviour.

Mr Clyde shrugged and smiled. "Yes."

* * *

Mr Melamed did not inquire further into how the matter with Mr Waters was resolved. He respected the silence that Mr Powell had wrapped about his private affairs, and when they met it was to play a game of chess or discuss a property that they thought to sell or buy. However, not long afterward, Mr Melamed received a letter from a well-known jeweller who had recently made a most interesting purchase. The jeweller, aware of Mr Melamed's interest in fine gems, invited Mr Melamed to see the jewels. Mr Melamed went, recognized the stunning sapphire and diamond set of necklace, earrings, bracelet and ring as formerly belonging to his friend, Mr Powell, and purchased the set on the spot. He did not tell Mr Powell what he had done; he knew that his friend would never accept the jewels as a gift, since no man who valued his personal honour wished to be in the debt of another. But Mr Melamed thought that if he would present the jewels as a gift on Thomas Powell's wedding day, whenever that happy day might occur, that the jewels might be successfully restored to their former owner under that guise.

As for Lady Marblehead, that lady returned to her former frugal ways, but it was said that she enjoyed her little economies less than before. It is one thing to play the part of a widow in reduced circumstances and quite another to actually be one. Yet to her surprise, she discovered that her tragedy had made her heir, Thomas Powell, more sympathetic to her condition. Although he could not send her little presents, he did write to her from Portugal with more frequency. Whether this was due to "misery loves company" or reasons more sublime, this Author cannot say.

Mr Clyde, however, soon departed from Mayfair and Lady Marblehead's life. She had made a gift to him of the pearl bracelet, after informing him that she had made a new will after all, and he could expect to inherit nothing else under the terms of that document. Perhaps he did as he once mentioned, and sold the bracelet and moved to the Continent. Again, this Author cannot say. She can only recommend that should you, dear Reader, encounter Mr Clyde in your own journeys through life, beware!

Mr Lazer Amos also disappeared, and took Mr Melamed's ten pounds with him. The factory where he had made his loathsome brew was shut down and the unsold store of tea leaves burned, as Mr Melamed had promised.

Mr Baruch Amos, it was revealed, had no idea that his brother, who had once studied to be a chemist but had gotten into some trouble with the law, had returned to his old ways. Instead, he believed with a brother's love Lazer's assurances that he had every intention of earning his daily bread in an honest fashion. Mr Baruch Amos was therefore truly shocked that his tea might cause harm, and begged Mr Melamed to believe that his remorse was genuine. Mr Melamed did believe the man, and he gave Mr Amos a gift of ten pounds to set himself up in a new business endeavour, with the stipulation that this business should not involve food.

And what of little Ezekiel, you may wonder? If, Reader, you have ever heard of something that we Jews call a *Seudas Hoda'ah*, a meal of thanksgiving, you may guess the rest of this story. That joyous meal was held at a certain house on Devonshire Square, where the Lyon family had invited several guests for dinner. Mr Melamed was there, of course, as were Mr and Mrs Franks and their daughter Harriet. Mr and Mrs Baer had closed early their kosher establishment in the City, so that they and their brood of children could attend as well. Mr and Mrs Goldsmith, and their son Isaac, were also at the table.

Other guests included Mr Taylor and Miss Taylor, who had been restored to their former happy selves now that the crisis was over. Their grandfather, Mr Jeremiah Schneider, who looked quite a different man dressed as he was in a new suit of clothes, sat beside them, and while the guests waited for the meal to begin it was revealed that in his younger years Mr Schneider had been a man of business with a comfortable livelihood. Then the Wheel of Fortune turned and he lost it all, a circumstance that had forced him to take up the profession of an old clothes man.

But where was the guest of honour?

Mrs Lyon, worried that her soup might burn, inquired of Mr Melamed if he knew when that person would arrive.

"I am sure it will be soon," he replied. "I sent my carriage to bring him and the others."

And, indeed, just a few minutes later — and, happily, before the soup did burn — the door to the Lyons' dining room was opened and a small procession came inside. First to enter the room were the Earl of Gravel Lane and General Well'ngone, who tried to pretend, with their accustomed aplomb, that they were invited to dinner parties every night of the week and always arrived there by carriage.

After them, came Simon and the guest of honour, little Ezekiel, who both had been given new suits of clothing for the occasion. Although Ezekiel was looking much better than the last time we saw him, in the pages of this book, the truth was that he still looked rather pale and thin. However, Simon assured the anxious crowd that Ezekiel was truly on his way to a full recovery.

"Last night Ezekiel told me that he felt strong enough to continue with his lessons, and I have introduced him to the letter B," said Simon. "I have every expectation that he shall be a master of this letter before summer."

After the other guests expressed their joy and satisfaction upon hearing this happy news, the soup was served. Then Mr Taylor decided that it was an appropriate time for him to share some good news of his own. "I have been offered an excellent position as a physician in Manchester," he said. "Mr Schneider, Miss Taylor, and I intend to move there next month."

"We are all happy for you, I am sure," said Mr Lyon, "although the children at the orphanage will be sorry to lose you. Are you certain we cannot convince you to stay?"

"It is very good of you to offer, Mr Lyon, but it is better that I make a fresh start somewhere else. People will always associate me with the outbreak of that stomach illness, whether they wish to or not."

"Then let us all drink a toast to your success in Manchester, Mr Taylor, and to your good health."

Mrs Baer, who was seated next to Mrs Lyon, gave her hostess a knowing look. Mrs Lyon, whose thoughts, now that the soup had been served, had turned to the roast and the dismal possibility that it might have become too dried out, gave a puzzled look in return.

"Manchester," Mrs Baer whispered. "Manchester!"

"Yes, I heard. What about it?"

"Mr Oppenheim is in Manchester," said Mrs Baer, casting yet another knowing look, this time in the direction of Miss Elisheva Taylor, as she held her napkin in her hands in such a way that it resembled a marriage canopy.

"Oh," said Mrs Lyon, with an air of great understanding.

Then the two ladies raised their glasses as one and said, "To Manchester! *L'chayim!*"

THE END

ABOUT THE AUTHOR

Libi Astaire is an award-winning author who often writes about Jewish history. In addition to her Jewish Regency Mystery Series featuring Ezra Melamed, General Well'ngone and the Earl of Gravel Lane, she is the author of the novel *Terra Incognita*, about modern-day descendants of Spain's crypto-Jews, *The Banished Heart*, about William Shakespeare's writing of *The Merchant of Venice*, and several volumes of Chassidic tales. She lives in Jerusalem, Israel.

For updates about future books, visit her website at www.libiastaire.weebly.com.

GET COZY WITH
ANOTHER GREAT
JEWISH REGENCY MYSTERY

The Moon Taker

In this second volume of the Jewish Regency Mystery Series, General Well'ngone and the Earl of Gravel Lane set out to discover who murdered Mr. Hamburg, a colleague of theirs in the secondhand linen trade. But before they can unmask the killer, they must unravel the secret of a mysterious snuff box—a quest that takes them from their East End slum to an elegant country house where a group of distinguished astronomers are meeting.

The Doppelganger's Dance
"Another great read by Libi Astaire" — Amazon.com

A young Jewish violinist and composer comes to Regency London to find fame and fortune, but disaster strikes when someone steals his compositions before he can publish and perform them. He therefore turns to Mr. Melamed for help with finding the thief--and thus begins one of the most discomposing mysteries of the wealthy-widower-turned-sleuth's career.

Too Many Coins

When an ancient coin from the Land of Israel goes missing during a dinner party hosted by the Lyon family, the most likely suspect is Judah Birnbaum, a young man from the Holy Land who has come to England to raise funds for his community in Safed. But why would the young man jeopardize his mission by stealing the coin? In this novella, Mr. Melamed for once has too many clues—which makes the matter of the missing coin one of the most wholly baffling cases of his career.

General Well'ngone in Love

In this novella set during the Frost Fair of 1814, a recently orphaned boy disappears, seemingly off the face of the earth. Mr. Melamed enlists the aid of General Well'ngone, a young Jewish pickpocket, who has his own reason for wishing to find the missing child—the General has fallen in love with the boy's older sister.

Made in the USA
Middletown, DE
19 February 2015